FRANKENSTEIN

GOLD EDITION

MARY SHELLEY

EDITED BY
ADAPTIVE READER

ISBN: 979-8-8692-9609-2 (Paperback)

CONTENTS

INTRODUCTION

Welcome to Adaptive Reader, your portal to the captivating world of literature, tailored to fit your unique reading abilities.

In today's fast-paced and diverse learning environment, we believe in the power of personalized learning experiences. That's where the concept of leveled reading comes in, and why we, at Adaptive Reader, have dedicated ourselves to offering a broad collection of classic novels at various reading levels. Our mission is to make the joy and benefits of reading accessible to everyone.

THE BENEFITS OF LEVELED TEXTS

So, what exactly is leveled reading? It's an approach that matches students with texts that align with their unique reading abilities. This ensures that every reader is challenged just the right amount - enough to grow, but not so much that they feel overwhelmed or frustrated.

For students, this means you'll engage with texts that stretch your reading skills while keeping the experience enjoyable and manageable. You'll gain confidence as you successfully comprehend each level and feel motivated to explore more challenging texts as your reading skills grow.

For teachers, Adaptive Reader provides a valuable tool to support differentiated instruction. You can assign the same novel to your entire class while ensuring each student reads a version that aligns with their reading level. This allows all students to participate in class discussions and activities, fostering a more inclusive learning environment.

For parents, Adaptive Reader offers a supportive tool to encourage your children's reading journey. As your child progresses through the different levels of a novel, they'll not only enhance their reading skills but also develop a deeper love for literature.

READING ACROSS MULTIPLE EDITIONS

All of our leveled novels include passage markers that correspond to the same content across every one of our editions. This means that passage '62' in our silver edition contains the same themes and plot elements as passage '62' in our original edition.

For teachers, this means that you can say "let's look at passage 35 together. What is the author trying to tell us here?" and all of your students will be reading the same content — but with vocabulary and syntax that's adapted to their reading level.

Our online reading tool, available at www.adaptivereader.com, gives students and teachers free access to the original text with passage markers. We encourage teachers to include close readings of the original text as part of their coursework, giving all students exposure to the rich original syntax and language of these exceptional authors.

THE POWER OF LITERATURE

At Adaptive Reader, we are committed to helping everyone experience the power of literature. So whether you're a student diving into a classic novel, a teacher looking for flexible resources, or a parent seeking ways to support your child's literacy, Adaptive Reader is here for you.

We invite you to embark on this exciting literary journey with us. Enjoy the world of stories, characters, and ideas that await you in our collection of leveled novels. Happy reading!

LETTER I

To Mrs. Saville, England.

St. Petersburgh, December 11th, 17--.

I'm happy to share with you that everything is going well with the beginning of the project you've been worried about. I just got here yesterday, and my first job is to tell my dear sister that I'm doing fine and feeling more and more confident that my plans will work.

I'm already very far north of London and as I walk in the streets of Petersburgh, I feel a chilly breeze on my face that makes me feel invigorated and happy. Do you know what I mean? This breeze has come from the places I'm heading towards, and it gives me a taste of the cold climates there. It makes me even more excited and vivid in my daydreams. I can't convince myself that the pole is only a place of frost and emptiness. In my mind, it's a region of beauty and joy. Margaret, the sun is always visible there, its large round shape just on the edge of the horizon, spreading light forever. And, if I can trust what earlier explorers have said, there is no snow or frost there. Instead, we can sail across calm waters to a land that surpasses everything we've ever discovered before in terms of wonders and beauty. The things that exist there, and the way the heavenly bodies function, will be like nothing we've ever seen before in these unexplored lands. Just imagine what we might find in a place that's always filled with light! Maybe I'll even discover the amazing force that attracts compass needles, and I might be able to make sense of all the strange movements of the planets. I'll finally satisfy my burning curiosity by seeing a part of the world no one has ever seen before, and I might walk on ground that's never been touched by anyone else. These are the things that interest me, and they're enough to make me forget all fear of danger or death. They're the reason I'm starting this difficult journey with the same joy a child feels when embarking on an adventure with friends in a little boat on a river. But even if all my hopes and ideas turn out to be false, you can't deny the incredible benefit I'll bring to all humanity, both now and in future generations, by discovering a shortcut near the pole to these countries that currently take months to reach. Or by figuring out the secret of the magnet, which can only be done by carrying out an undertaking like mine, if it's even possible at all.

These thoughts have calmed my initial restlessness and now I feel an intense excitement that lifts my spirit to the sky. Having a clear purpose brings great peace to the mind, allowing it to focus on a single goal. This journey has always been my favorite dream since I was young. I devoured the stories of countless expeditions that aimed to reach the North Pacific Ocean by sailing through the polar seas. Perhaps you recall how Uncle Thomas's library consisted solely of books about these voyages. I may not have had a proper education, but I was consumed by a deep love for reading. Those volumes were my constant companions, and my familiarity with them only intensified the sorrow I felt as a child when I learned that my father's dying wish had forbidden Uncle Thomas from allowing me to pursue a life at sea.

These dreams faded away when I discovered the works of poets whose words enchanted my soul and transported it to the heavens. I, too, became a poet and for a year, I lived in a paradise of my own creation, imagining that I, too, could claim a place among the greats like Homer and Shakespeare. You know well of my ultimate failure and the weight of disappointment I carried on my shoulders. Yet, just when hope seemed lost, I unexpectedly inherited my cousin's fortune, and my thoughts turned back to my original passion.

Six years have gone by since I made the decision to do what I'm doing now. I can still remember the moment when I committed myself to this important endeavor. I began by toughening up my body. I went on several trips to the North Sea with the people who hunt for whales, enduring the cold, hunger, thirst, and lack of sleep willingly. During the day, I often worked harder than the regular sailors, and at night, I dedicated my time to studying math, medicine theory, and other parts of science that a sailor could benefit from the most. Twice, I even worked as a lower-ranking officer on a whaling ship in Greenland, and I did a great job. I must admit, I felt a little proud when my captain offered me the second highest position on the ship and begged me to stay because he thought my work was so valuable.

Now, my dear Margaret, don't you think I deserve to achieve something great? I could have lived a life of comfort and luxury, but I chose fame over all the temptations that money could bring. Oh, if only someone would answer with encouragement! My bravery and determination are strong, but my hopes go up and down, and my mood often gets low. I'm getting ready to go on a long and difficult journey that will require a lot of courage. Not only will I have to lift the spirits of others, but sometimes I'll have to keep myself going when they start to lose hope.

This is the most favorable time to travel in Russia. They travel quickly over the snow in their sledges, which is enjoyable and, in my opinion, more pleasant than riding in an English stage-coach. The cold is not too extreme if you wear fur clothing - something I have already started doing. There is a big difference between walking on a ship's deck and staying seated for hours, where lack of movement allows the blood to freeze in your veins. I have no desire to risk my life on the road between St. Petersburg and Archangel.

I will leave for Archangel in two or three weeks, and my plan is to hire a ship there. It shouldn't be difficult to do so by paying for the owner's insurance. I will also recruit enough sailors experienced in whale-fishing. I don't intend to sail until June, and as for when I will return... Ah, dear sister, how can I answer that? If I succeed, many months, or perhaps years, will pass before we can see each other again. If I fail, I may see you again soon, or never.

Farewell, my dear and wonderful Margaret. May blessings rain down upon you and protect me, so that I can express my gratitude to you again and again for your love and kindness.

With affection,

R. Walton.

LETTER 2

To Mrs. Saville, England.

Archangel, March 28, 17—.

Time seems to move so slowly here, surrounded by freezing temperatures and snow! However, I have made progress towards my goal. I have found a ship to hire and I am in the process of gathering my sailors. The ones I have already recruited seem reliable and brave.

But there is one thing that I've never been able to satisfy, and the absence of it is now causing me great distress. I don't have a friend, Margaret. When I am filled with the excitement of success, there will be no one to share in my joy. If I am faced with disappointment, no one will try to comfort me. I will put my thoughts down on paper, it is true. However, that's not a satisfactory way to express my feelings. I long for the companionship of someone who could understand me; someone whose eyes would respond to mine. You may think I'm being overly imaginative, my dear sister, but I deeply feel the need for a friend. I have no one near me who is both gentle and brave, someone who is knowledgeable and has an open mind, whose interests align with my own, who could support or improve my plans. How would such a friend help me correct my mistakes! I am too eager to act, and too impatient with challenges. But it is an even greater problem that I am self-taught. For the first fourteen years of my life, I spent my time freely on the common, and only read our uncle Thomas's books on voyages. It wasn't until I reached that age that I discovered the works of our country's celebrated poets; but it was too late for me to fully benefit from this realization, and only then did I realize the importance of learning languages beyond my own. Now I am twenty-eight, and I am actually more uneducated than many fifteen-year-old schoolboys. It is true that I have thought deeply and have grand dreams, but they are unfinished and unrefined. For that reason, I am in great need of a friend who would have the wisdom not to dismiss me as idealistic, and who would care enough about me to try to shape my thinking.

8   Well, these are useless complaints. I shall certainly find no friend on the wide ocean among merchants and sailors. Yet some feelings do seem to be enchoed in others. My lieutenant, for instance, is a man of wonderful courage and enterprise; he is madly desirous of glory and advancement in his profession. He is an Englishman. I first became acquainted with him on board a whale vessel. He was unemployed in this city, I easily engaged him to assist in my enterprise.

9   The captain is a person with a great personality, known on the ship for being gentle and having a calm approach to discipline. These qualities, along with his honesty and bravery, made me really want to hire him. Growing up in isolation and spending my formative years under the care of kind and gentle women, I developed a strong distaste for the typical harshness seen on board a ship. I never believed it was necessary. So when I heard about a sailor who was known for his kindness and the respect his crew had for him, I knew I was lucky to have him on my team. I first heard about him in a rather romantic way from a woman whose life he had made happy. Here is his story. Several years ago, he loved a young Russian woman who had modest means. He had accumulated a significant amount of money from winning prizes at sea, and the girl's father agreed to

their marriage. He met his bride-to-be once before the wedding and found her in tears, begging him not to go through with it. She confessed that she loved someone else, but he was poor and her father would never approve of their union. In an act of generosity, my friend decided to let her go. He had already purchased a farm with his earnings, planning to spend the rest of his life there. However, he gave it all to his rival, as well as the remaining prize money, so that they could buy livestock and start a life together. He then approached the young woman's father to ask for his consent for her to marry her true love. But the father was steadfast in his refusal, feeling obligated to my friend. Unable to change his mind, my friend left the country and didn't return until he heard that his former love had married the man of her choice. "What an honorable man!" you might say. And he truly is. However, he has had little education and is very quiet, with a kind of unintentional carelessness that both makes his actions more surprising and takes away from the interest and sympathy that he would otherwise evoke.

Don't think that my occasional complaints or my ability to find solace in my struggles means I am unsure about my decisions. Those are as firm as can be, and my journey is only delayed until the weather allows me to set sail. This winter has been incredibly harsh, but the signs of spring are promising, and it seems to be arriving earlier than usual. So, I might be able to depart sooner than I anticipated. I won't act recklessly - you know me well enough to trust that I am wise and thoughtful when it comes to the safety of others in my care.

I can't really explain how I feel about the upcoming journey. It's hard to describe the mix of excitement and fear that's taking over me as I get ready to leave. I'm heading towards unknown lands, to places that are full of mystery and uncertainty. But don't worry, I won't make any dangerous mistakes that could put my life in danger. I won't come back to you like the miserable sailor in the poem "The Ancient Mariner." While it may seem as thought I'm making a joke, I have a secret to confess. I think my fascination with the dangerous and mysterious aspects of the ocean is influenced by the works of poets. There's something inside me that I can't quite explain. I'm a hardworking person, always putting in the effort and dedication, but there's also a part of me that craves adventure and believes in the extraordinary. It pushes me to venture beyond the ordinary paths and explore the untamed sea and unvisited places.

But now let's talk about more important things. Will we see each other again, after I sail across vast oceans and return from the southernmost tip of Africa or America? I don't want to get my hopes up, but I can't bear to think of the opposite outcome. Please keep writing to me whenever you can. Your letters might reach me when I need them the most to lift my spirits. I care deeply for you. Remember me fondly, even if you never receive a letter from me again.

With love,

Robert Walton.

LETTER 3

Dear Mrs. Saville, England.

Hi, Sister. July 7th, 17—.

I'm writing this hurried note to let you know that I'm safe and making good progress on my journey. This letter will reach England on a ship that's heading back from Archangel. They're luckier than me because I might not see our homeland for many years. But I'm feeling positive! My crew is brave and determined, and they're not intimidated by the floating ice that keeps passing by, warning us of the dangers ahead. We've already reached a really high latitude, but it's summertime here, and even though it's not as warm as in England, the southern winds are pushing us closer to the shores I'm so eager to reach, and they bring a bit of unexpected warmth.

Nothing eventful has happened so far that's worth mentioning in a letter. We've had a couple of strong winds and a small leak, but experienced sailors don't even consider those as noteworthy accidents. I'll be satisfied if nothing worse happens to us during the voyage.

Goodbye, my dear Margaret. I promise you, I won't recklessly put myself or anyone else in danger. I'll stay calm, determined, and cautious.

14 But I will succeed in my efforts. Why not? So far, I have traveled confidently across the vast oceans, with even the stars themselves bearing witness to my triumph. Why shouldn't I continue journeying over the wild, yet submissive, waters? What could possibly hinder the determined heart and resolute will of a person?

My heart fills with emotion as I express these thoughts. But I must bring this letter to a close. May heaven bless my dear sister!

R. W.

LETTER 4

To Mrs. Saville, England.

August 5th, 17—.

Something really strange happened to us, and I just have to write it down, even though it's likely you'll see me before you get these papers.

On Monday (July 31st), we were almost trapped by ice. It surrounded the ship on all sides, leaving very little room for it to float freely. Our situation was pretty dangerous, especially because a thick fog enclosed us too. So, we decided to stay put, hoping that the weather would change.

Around two o'clock, the fog cleared and we saw huge and uneven plains of ice stretching out in every direction. It felt like they would go on forever. Some of my friends groaned, and I started feeling worried too, but then we noticed something strange and forgot about our own problems. We saw a small carriage, attached to a sled and pulled by dogs, heading towards the north about half a mile away. In the carriage was a figure who looked like a man, but really tall. He was steering the dogs. Using our telescopes, we watched the traveler quickly move away until he disappeared among the distant bumps in the ice.

This sight amazed us greatly. We believed we were hundreds of miles from any land, yet this sighting suggested otherwise. However, since we were trapped by ice, we couldn't follow his path, which we had observed carefully.

About two hours later, we heard the sounds of the sea and by nightfall, the ice broke, freeing our ship. However, we decided to wait until morning before continuing, fearing the large, loose chunks of ice that float after the breaking of the ice. During this time, I took the opportunity to rest for a few hours.

When morning came and it was light outside, I went on deck and saw the sailors gathered on one side of the ship, apparently talking to someone in the sea. It turned out to be another sled, similar to the one we had seen before, which had drifted towards us overnight on a large piece of ice. Only one dog was alive, but inside the sled was a person whom the sailors were trying to convince to come aboard the ship. Unlike the other traveler who seemed like a wild inhabitant of an unknown island, this person was European. When the sailors saw me, the captain said, "Here is our captain, and he won't let you die at sea."

When the stranger saw me, he spoke to me in English, albeit with a foreign accent. "Before I come on board your ship," he said, "could you please tell me where you are headed?"

I was incredibly surprised when the man on the edge of destruction asked me such a question. It seemed unbelievable that he wouldn't see my vessel as a sanctuary, worth more than any treasure on earth. Regardless, I told him that we were on a voyage to explore the northern pole.

He seemed to be satisfied upon hearing this and agreed to come on board. Oh, Margaret, if only you could have seen the condition of the man who struck this deal to save himself. His limbs were nearly frozen, and he looked horribly weak and thin from exhaustion and suffering. I had never seen someone in such a miserable state. We tried to carry him to the cabin, but as soon as he left the fresh air, he passed out. So, we brought him back to the deck and revived him by rubbing him with brandy and making him drink a little. Once he showed signs of life, we wrapped him in blankets and placed him near the kitchen stove to warm up. Slowly but surely, he regained his strength and ate some soup, which did wonders for him.

For two days, he remained unable to speak, and I worried that his suffering had affected his sanity. Once he started to recover, I moved him to my cabin and took care of him as much as I could. He was a fascinating person to observe. His eyes often carried a look of wildness or even madness, but there were moments when a small act of kindness or help would light up his entire face with warmth and kindness that I have never seen before. However, he mostly seemed desolate and hopeless, at times gritting his teeth in frustration from the weight of his burdens.

When my guest started to regain his strength, I had to do my best to keep the crew from bombarding him with questions. I refused to let their idle curiosity disturb him, knowing fully well that his recovery depended on complete rest for both his body and mind. But one time, the lieutenant couldn't resist asking why he had traveled so far on the ice in such a strange vehicle.

Suddenly, his expression turned dark, and he replied, "To find someone who ran away from me."

"And did this person you were pursuing also travel in the same way?"

"Yes."

"In that case, I believe we may have seen him. The day before we rescued you, we spotted a group of dogs pulling a sled with a man on it, crossing the ice."

The stranger became interested when the lieutenant mentioned the creature, whom he referred to as a "daemon," and began asking many questions about its path. Later, when we were alone, he said to me, "I'm sure I have piqued your curiosity, as well as the curiosity of these kind people, but you are too thoughtful to pry."

"Indeed, it would be impolite and unkind of me to burden you with my inquiries," I replied.

"Yet you saved me from a strange and dangerous situation. You have kindly brought me back to life."

Afterwards, he asked me if I thought the breaking of the ice had destroyed the other sled. I couldn't give a definitive answer, as the ice didn't break until close to midnight, and the traveler may have reached safety before then, but I couldn't be sure.

From that moment on, a newfound energy infused the stranger's body. He eagerly wanted to be on deck to look for the sled that had appeared earlier, but I convinced him to stay in the cabin, as he was too weak to endure the harshness of the outside air. I assured him that someone would keep watch and immediately inform him if any new object came into view.

This is my record of what has happened with this strange event up until now. The stranger has been getting healthier, but is very quiet and uncomfortable when anyone other than me goes into his room. However, he is so polite and kind that the sailors are all interested in him, even though they haven't really talked to him much. Personally, I am starting to love him like a brother; his constant and deep sadness makes me feel sympathy and compassion. He must have been an amazing person in his better days, and even now he is wrecked but still attractive and kind.

I mentioned in one of my letters, dear Margaret, that I wouldn't find any friends out on the vast ocean. But I have found a man who, before he was broken by misery, I would have been happy to have as my brother in a heartbeat.

I will continue writing about the stranger every now and then, if there are any new events to write about.

August 13th, 17—.

My affection for my guest grows stronger every day. He both amazes and saddens me to an incredible degree. How can I watch such an admirable person be destroyed by sadness without feeling deeply saddened myself? He is so gentle, yet so wise. His mind is well-educated and when he speaks, even though he chooses his words carefully, they flow quickly and with unmatched eloquence.

He has now recovered from his illness and spends most of his time on the deck, eagerly looking out for the sledge that came before his own. Although he is unhappy, he still finds interest in the endeavors of others. He has engaged in conversations with me about my own projects, which I have shared with him openly. He attentively listened to my arguments for why I believe I will succeed and took note of every detail I shared about my preparations. His empathy towards me encouraged me to express my intense passion and the lengths I am willing to go to achieve my goals. I confessed that I would gladly sacrifice my wealth, my life, and all my hopes for the advancement of my venture. The value of one person's life seemed small when compared to the knowledge and power I hoped to gain over the obstacles that threaten humanity. As I spoke, a shadow fell over my companion's face. I could tell he was trying to hide his emotions, as he covered his eyes with his hands. My voice trembled and faltered as tears streamed from between his fingers, and a pained groan escaped from his chest. I paused, waiting for him to speak. Finally, in a broken voice, he uttered, "Unfortunate man! Do you also share my madness? Have you also partaken in the intoxicating drink? Listen to me - allow me to share my story, and you will surely turn away from that cup."

He had gone through a difficult time and was now recovering from his illness. He spent a lot of time on deck, as if he was waiting for a sledge that came before his own. Despite his unhappiness, he showed interest in the projects of others. He often talked to me about mine, and I shared all the details with him. He listened carefully and understood why I believed in the success of my project. I spoke from my heart, expressing my passion and willingness to sacrifice everything for it. I believed that even a person's life was worth sacrificing for the sake of knowledge and power over our enemies. As I spoke, his face darkened. He tried to hide his emotions, but tears streamed down his face. He spoke in a broken voice, calling me an unhappy man and urging me to abandon my pursuit.

23   Even though he is feeling broken and downcast, he still has a deep appreciation for the beauty of nature. The starry sky, the sea, and all the breathtaking sights of this amazing place seem to lift his spirit and transport his soul. In a way, he has two lives: one filled with sorrow and disappointment, and another where he retreats within himself and becomes like a celestial being, untouched by grief or foolishness.

I can't help but be enthusiastic when I talk about this extraordinary traveler. If you saw him, you wouldn't be able to resist him either. You have been educated and refined by books and a life away from the chaos of the world, which makes you more discerning. This quality in you makes you perfect to recognize the exceptional qualities of this remarkable man. I have often tried to figure out what it is about him that sets him so far apart from anyone else I have ever known. I think it's his instinctive understanding, his ability to judge quickly but accurately, and his knack for uncovering the true causes of things with remarkable clarity and precision. On top of that, he has the gift of eloquence and a voice with such a range of tones that it's like music that captivates the soul.

August 19. 17—.

24   Yesterday the stranger told me, "You can see, Captain Walton, that I have experienced great and unprecedented misfortunes. I had decided, at one point, that these evils should be forgotten with my death. However, you have convinced me to change my mind. You are seeking knowledge and wisdom, as I once did, and I sincerely hope that the fulfillment of your desires will not be a source of harm to you, as it has been for me. I don't know if sharing the story of my disasters will be helpful to you. But when I consider that you are following the same path, exposing yourself to the same dangers that have shaped me, I believe that you can glean a fitting moral from my tale. It may guide you if you succeed in your mission, and bring you solace in the event of failure. Be prepared to hear about

extraordinary happenings. If we were in less dramatic surroundings, I might fear encountering your doubt, and even mockery. Yet, in these untamed and mysterious regions, many things will seem possible that would provoke laughter in those unfamiliar with the ever-changing abilities of nature. Moreover, I have no doubt that my story provides clear evidence of the truthfulness of the events it contains."

I was very pleased to receive the offer to communicate, but I couldn't bear to let him revisit his grief by recounting his misfortunes. I was extremely eager to hear the promised story, partly out of curiosity and partly out of a strong desire to improve his situation if I had the ability to do so. I expressed these sentiments in my response.

"I appreciate your sympathy," he replied, "but it is futile and my destiny is almost fulfilled. I am only waiting for one event, and then I will find peace. I understand your intentions," he continued, noticing that I wanted to interrupt him, "but you are mistaken, my friend, if you allow me to call you that. Nothing can change my fate. Listen to my story, and you will see how firmly it is set."

He told me that he would start telling his story the next day when I had free time. I was very grateful for this promise. Each night, when I don't have important obligations, I've decided to record his words as accurately as I can. If I'm busy, I'll at least take some notes. This manuscript will surely bring you great pleasure. But for me, who knows him and hears it directly from him, how interested and sympathetic I will be when I read it in the future! Even now, as I begin my task, I can still hear his deep voice in my ears. His shining eyes look at me with a mix of sadness and sweetness. I see his thin hand raised in excitement, while his face reflects the passion within him. His story must be strange and disturbing. The storm that attacked the brave ship on its journey, causing it to crash like this, must have been terrifying.

CHAPTER

ONE

27 I COME from Geneva and my family is well-known in the city. My ancestors held important positions as counselors and public officials. My father was highly respected for his honesty and dedication to serving the public. He devoted his youth to the affairs of our country, and it was only later in life that he got married and had children.

28 Allow me to share the story of my father's marriage, as it reveals his notable character. One of his closest friends, a merchant named Beaufort, experienced a series of unfortunate events that led to him to poverty. It pained my father to witness Beaufort's suffering, as he was a proud and dignified man who detested living in such a way after having once held a prominent position in society. Beaufort, true to his honorable nature, repaid all his debts and sought safety with his daughter in the town of Lucerne, where they lived in isolation and misery. My father cherished his friendship with Beaufort and was deeply saddened by his friend's unfortunate circumstances. He felt great sorrow when Beaufort decided to sever ties with society. Without hesitation, my father set out to find him, hoping to convince him to start afresh by extending his own credit and assistance.

29   Beaufort had made sure to hide himself well, and it took my father ten months to find out where he was living. My father was thrilled when he finally found the house, which was in a poor neighborhood near the Reuss river. But when he walked in, all he found was misery and despair. Beaufort had managed to save a small amount of money from his previous wealth, enough to provide for himself for a few months. During that time, he hoped to find a decent job working for a merchant. However, those months were spent doing nothing, and his grief only grew deeper and more painful as he had time to think. Eventually, his mental and physical health declined so much that after three months he was bedridden and unable to do anything.

Beaufort's daughter, Caroline, took care of him with great love and care. But she could see that their limited money was running out quickly, and there were no other means of support. However, Caroline had an extraordinary mind and a strong spirit, so she found ways to earn some money. She did simple tasks like sewing and weaving straw, doing whatever she could to earn just enough to survive.

30   Several months went by in this way. Her father's condition worsened, so she had to spend even more time taking care of him. The money she had to live on started to run out, and by the tenth month, her father passed away with her holding onto him. She was left completely alone and without any means of support. This final tragedy was too much for her to bear, and she knelt beside Beaufort's coffin, crying uncontrollably. It was at that moment that my father walked into the room. He came to her like a guardian angel, offering to take care of the young girl. After Beaufort's burial, he escorted her to Geneva and found a relative who could provide her with protection. Two years later, Caroline became his wife.

31   My parents had a significant age difference, but it only brought them closer in a strong and devoted love. My father valued justice, which made it important for him to deeply approve and love. Perhaps he had experienced heartbreak in the past, realizing the

unworthiness of someone he once loved, and it made him appreciate genuine worth even more. His attachment to my mother was filled with gratitude and adoration, different from the affection of old age. It was rooted in admiration for her virtues and a desire to make up for the sorrows she had endured. He catered to her every wish and made sure she was comfortable. He protected her like a delicate flower, shielding her from any hardships, and surrounding her with things that brought her joy. The challenges my mother had faced had taken a toll on her health and her once serene spirit. In the two years leading up to their marriage, my father gradually left behind his public responsibilities. After they got married, they decided to travel to Italy, seeking the pleasant climate and the change of scenery as a way to restore her weakened body.

They traveled to Germany and France after Italy. I was born in Naples and went with them as a baby on their adventures. I was their only child for many years. Even though they loved each other very much, they seemed to have endless love to shower upon me. My first memories are of my mother's gentle hugs and my father's kind smile when he looked at me. I was their toy and their most precious possession. But I was also more than that — I was their child, a innocent and vulnerable being given to them by Heaven. They had the power to guide my life towards happiness or misery depending on how well they fulfilled their responsibilities towards me. With the deep understanding of their duty to their beloved child, along with their loving nature, I experienced patience, kindness, and self-control from them at every moment of my early life. They guided me with care and it felt like every moment was filled with joy.

When I was young, I was the only focus of my parents' attention. My mother had wished for a daughter, but I remained their only child. When I was around five years old, we took a trip outside of Italy and stayed by Lake Como for a week. My parents had a kind nature, so they often visited the homes of the less fortunate. It wasn't just an obligation for my mother. It was a necessity, a passion to help those in need, considering the hardships she had endured in her own life. During one of our walks, we came across a poor cottage in a secluded valley. The sight was desolate, and the presence of several underdressed children hinted at extreme poverty. One day, while my father was away in Milan, my mother and I decided to visit this humble dwelling. Inside, we found a hardworking peasant couple, exhausted from their struggles, barely able to provide a meager meal for their five hungry children. Among them, one child caught my mother's attention the most. She seemed different from the others - fair-skinned and delicate. Despite her worn-out clothes, her golden hair shone brightly, making her stand out. Her face was angelic, with a clear forehead, flawless blue eyes, and lips that revealed her sensitivity and kindness. Anyone who saw her couldn't help but recognize her as someone special, someone who seemed to be sent from heaven with a divine aura surrounding her.

34   The kind peasant woman noticed that my mother was captivated by this beautiful young girl and eagerly shared her history. The girl was not their biological child, but the daughter of a nobleman from Milan. Her mother, who was German, sadly passed away during childbirth. The infant was then entrusted to the care of these kind people. At that time, the peasant couple was in a better financial situation. They had recently gotten married and had just welcomed their own first child. The girl's father was an Italian who deeply believed in restoring Italy's former glory and fought for its independence. However, he fell victim to the country's weaknesses. It is unclear whether he had died or was still imprisoned in Austrian dungeons. His property was confiscated, leaving his daughter as an orphan and beggar. She remained with her foster parents, and in their humble home she blossomed like a beautiful rose among thorny brambles.

35   When my father came back from Milan, he discovered me playing with a child in the hallway of our house. This child was even more beautiful than a picture of a cherub. She seemed to emit brightness from her appearance and moved with a grace lighter than the agile chamois of the hills. The reason behind this unexpected visitor

became clear. With my father's permission, my mother convinced her humble guardians to let her take care of the child. The guardians had grown fond of the sweet orphan, and her presence had brought them joy. However, it would be unfair to her to keep her in poverty and need when she could be provided with a better life. The guardians sought advice from their village priest, and together they decided that Elizabeth Lavenza would become a member of my parents' household. She would be more than a sister to me. She became a beautiful and cherished companion.

Everyone adored Elizabeth. The strong and almost worshipful affection that everyone felt for her became my pride and joy as well. The night before she came to my house, my mother had jokingly said, "I have a lovely gift for Victor. He will have it tomorrow." And when, the following day, she presented Elizabeth to me as her promised gift, I took her words seriously and saw Elizabeth as mine. She was mine to protect, love, and care for. Any praises given to her, I accepted as if they were about something that belonged to me. We affectionately called each other cousin. No word or expression could fully capture the kind of relationship we shared. She was more than a sister to me, and she would be mine until death.

CHAPTER

TWO

37   We grew up together. There was less than a year between our ages. It goes without saying that we were unfamiliar with any kind of disagreements or arguments. Harmony was the essence of our friendship, and the differences in our personalities brought us closer. Elizabeth had a more calm and focused nature, while I, with all my enthusiasm, was capable of more intense concentration and had a deeper thirst for knowledge. She enjoyed immersing herself in the imaginative works of poets, and in the magnificent and awe-inspiring scenes that surrounded our home in Switzerland. There were the majestic shapes of mountains, the changing seasons, storms and tranquility, the stillness of winter and the lively chaos of our summers in the Alps. She found plenty of opportunities for admiration and joy. Meanwhile, I delighted in delving into the causes behind these impressive phenomena. The world was like a secret to me, one that I yearned to unravel. Curiosity, determined exploration to understand the hidden laws of nature, and the happiness I felt akin to ecstasy as they were unveiled to me, are some of the earliest feelings I can recall.

38   When my parents had another son, who was seven years

6

younger than me, they decided to settle down in our home country and give up their nomadic lifestyle. We had a house in Geneva and a country estate in Belrive, on the eastern shore of the lake, about a little over a mile away from the city. We mostly lived in the country, and my parents led a somewhat secluded life. I preferred to avoid large crowds and instead formed deep connections with only a few people. Therefore, I didn't pay much attention to my classmates in general, but I formed a close and lasting friendship with one of them. Henry Clerval was the son of a merchant from Geneva. He was a boy with exceptional talents and imagination. He loved adventure, challenges, and even risky situations for the sheer thrill of it. He was well-versed in tales of knights and romances. He enjoyed writing heroic songs and started crafting stories of enchantment and knightly quests. He even attempted to organize plays and masquerades, where the characters were inspired by the heroes of Roncesvalles, the knights of King Arthur's Round Table, and the brave warriors who fought to reclaim the holy sepulcher from the infidels.

I had a truly happy childhood that I believe no other person could have experienced. My parents were incredibly kind and indulgent, always ensuring that we had plenty of delights to enjoy. Unlike some families, who seemed to rule their children's lives based on their own whims, my parents were the ones who created and provided all the wonderful things we had. Whenever I spent time with other families, I couldn't help but realize how fortunate I was. It made me grateful.

I must admit, I had a fiery temperament at times, and my passions ran strong. However, instead of being drawn to typical childish activities, I had an intense thirst for knowledge. And not just any knowledge, but the secrets of the heavens and the earth. Whether it was the tangible aspects of the world or the hidden depths of nature and the enigmatic human soul, I was captivated by the physical truths of our world. The structure of languages, the intricacies of governments, and the politics of different states did not hold much appeal for me. My focus was on uncovering the mysteries that lay beneath the surface.

40   Meanwhile, Clerval focused on the moral aspects of life. He was interested in the actions and virtues of heroic individuals and wanted to leave his own mark on history. In our peaceful home, Elizabeth's saintly nature illuminated everything. We shared her empathy: her smile, her gentle voice, and the loving look in her eyes were always there to bless and inspire us. She personified love, softening and captivating us. I might have become withdrawn and rough in my studies due to my passionate nature, but she was there to calm me and instill her own kindness. And as for Clerval, could anything negative ever affect his noble spirit? Perhaps not. Yet, it's possible that he wouldn't have been as compassionate and considerate in his generous acts if Elizabeth hadn't shown him the true beauty of helping others, making it the purpose and goal of his ambitious endeavors.

41   I have great pleasure in remembering my childhood, before bad things happened and made me think only about myself instead of making a difference in the world. As I tell the story of my early life, I also want to share the events that led to my later misfortune. I want to understand why I became so passionate about natural philosophy, the science that has shaped my life. When I was thirteen, my family and I went on a trip to the baths near Thonon. The bad weather kept us indoors at an inn for a whole day. In that inn, I happened to find a book by Cornelius Agrippa. At first, I didn't care much about it, but as I read about his theories and the amazing facts he described, my interest quickly turned into excitement. It felt like a new understanding was dawning on me, and I couldn't contain my joy, so I told my father about it. However, my father glanced casually at the title of the book and dismissed it, saying, "Oh, Cornelius Agrippa! Please don't waste your time on that! It's not worth it."

42   If my father had simply explained to me that the ideas of Agrippa were outdated, I would have put the book aside and returned to my previous studies. Under those circumstances, my imagination would

have remained satisfied. Maybe I may have never had the fateful encounter that led to my downfall. Unfortunately, my father's quick judgment of the book did not give me confidence that he was familiar with its contents, so I eagerly continued reading.

When I got back home, my first priority was to get my hands on all the works by this author, as well as those by Paracelsus and Albertus Magnus. I read and studied with great delight, feeling like I had discovered hidden treasures that few knew about. I have always had a deep desire to uncover the mysteries of nature. Despite the hard work and incredible discoveries made by modern scientists, I always felt dissatisfied and unfulfilled after my studies. It is said that Sir Isaac Newton himself compared his understanding to that of a child collecting seashells beside the vast and unexplored ocean of truth. Even the other philosophers in various fields of science that I knew of appeared to me as beginners in their pursuit.

The uneducated peasant could observe the elements around him and understand how to use them practically. The most knowledgeable philosopher didn't know much more. They could dissect, analyze, and name things, but they had no understanding of the underlying reasons, not to mention the deeper layers of causes. I had marveled at the barriers and obstacles that seemed to prevent humans from entering the realm of nature's secrets, and foolishly, in my ignorance, I had complained.

But there were books, and there were men who knew more and delved deeper. I trusted in their knowledge and became their student. It may seem strange that this happened in the 18th century, but while I followed the standard education in Geneva, I taught myself a great deal about my favorite subjects. My father wasn't a scientific person, so I had to navigate my studies on my own. Under the guidance of my new teachers, I diligently pursued the search for the philosopher's stone and the elixir of life, but eventually, my focus shifted solely to the elixir. Wealth was not the main goal. Instead, I longed for the glory of discovering a way to eradicate disease from the human body and make humanity impervious to anything but a violent death.

45   Nor were these the only things I imagined. The idea of summoning spirits or demons was a popular concept in the books I enjoyed, and I eagerly sought to make it a reality. Whenever my attempts at incantations failed, I believed it was due to my own lack of experience rather than any fault in my teachers. So, for a while, I occupied myself with outdated theories, mixing contradictory ideas and struggling to make sense of a vast range of knowledge. I was guided by a passionate imagination and childish reasoning, until an accident changed the course of my thoughts.

When I was around fifteen years old, my family and I were living near Belrive when we witnessed a violent and terrifying thunderstorm. It approached from behind the Jura mountains, and thunder roared loudly from different parts of the sky. I stayed at the door, fascinated and delighted, watching the storm's progress. Suddenly, a stream of fire shot out from an old and beautiful oak tree, about twenty yards away from our house. As the blinding light disappeared, the oak tree was gone, leaving behind only a charred stump. The next morning, when we examined it, we found the tree shattered in a peculiar way. It wasn't broken into pieces by the lightning, but rather reduced to thin strips of wood. I had never seen anything so completely destroyed.

46   Before this, I had some knowledge of the basic principles of electricity. During that time, a man who was well-versed in natural philosophy was present with us. He was intrigued by the thunderstorm and took the opportunity to explain a new and astonishing theory about electricity and galvanism. His explanations overshadowed the ideas of Cornelius Agrippa, Albertus Magnus, and Paracelsus, who were previously the focus of my imagination. However, for some reason, the downfall of these men discouraged me from continuing my usual studies. It felt as if nothing could ever be truly known or understood. All the subjects that had captivated my attention for so long suddenly seemed worthless. In a sudden change of

mind, common among young people, I abandoned my previous interests and developed a strong dislike for a so-called science that lacked true understanding. In this state of mind, I turned to mathematics and other areas of study related to it, considering them to be grounded in solid knowledge and deserving of my attention.

Our souls are complex, and our wellbeing can be influenced by even the smallest factors. When I reflect on the past, it seems to me that this sudden change in my desires and willpower was like a divine intervention, a final attempt by my guardian angel to protect me from the looming disaster. This victory was signaled by an unusual sense of calm and joy that washed over me as I let go of my old studies. In this way, I was being taught to associate suffering with pursuing those studies and happiness with abandoning them.

It was a brave effort by the forces of goodness, but ultimately, it was ineffective. Destiny held too much power, and its unchangeable laws had already determined my complete downfall.

CHAPTER

THREE

⁴⁸ WHEN I TURNED SEVENTEEN, my parents decided that I should go to the university in Ingolstadt to further my education. Up until then, I had been attending schools in Geneva. However, my father believed it was important for me to experience different ways of life beyond my own country. We had set an early date for my departure, but just before that day could come, the first tragic event of my life happened. It seemed like a sign of the sorrow that lay ahead for me.

⁴⁹ Elizabeth had contracted the scarlet fever, and her illness was very serious. Many arguments were made to persuade my mother not to take care of her. At first, she gave in to our pleas, but when she learned that her beloved daughter's life was in danger, she couldn't control her worry anymore. She tended to Elizabeth's sick bed, and her careful attention defeated the illness. Elizabeth was saved, but the consequences of this unwise decision were fatal for my mother. On the third day, she also fell ill. Her fever came with alarming symptoms, and the doctors' expressions indicated the worst outcome. On her deathbed, my mother still showed her bravery and kindness. She joined Elizabeth's and my hands together and said, "My children, I had hoped for your happiness through your union.

Now, this hope will be your father's comfort. Elizabeth, my love, you must take care of my younger children in my place. I am sad to leave you all, even though I have been happy and loved. But these thoughts don't suit me. I will try to accept death cheerfully and hope to see you in another world."

She passed away peacefully, and even in death, her face showed affection. I don't need to explain how it feels when someone you love so deeply is taken from you. The emptiness that consumes your soul and the despair that shows on your face. It takes a long time for the mind to accept that the person we saw every day, who felt like a part of ourselves, is truly gone forever—that the sparkle in their eyes has vanished, and the sound of their voice, so familiar and dear, will never be heard again. These are the thoughts that occupy our minds in the first days, but as time goes on and we face the harsh reality of the loss, the true bitterness of grief sets in. Yet, who hasn't experienced the pain of losing someone dear? Why should I describe a sorrow that everyone has felt and will feel? Eventually, there comes a time when grief becomes more of a personal indulgence rather than a necessity. The smile that appears on our lips, though it may be seen as sacrilegious, is not banished. My mother was no longer with us, but we still had responsibilities to fulfill. We had to keep moving forward, alongside everyone else, and learn to consider ourselves fortunate as long as there was someone the destroyer hadn't taken away.

I was going to Ingolstadt, but I delayed my departure because of the recent events. My father gave me a few more weeks before I had to leave. It seemed wrong to leave so soon after the loss we experienced and dive back into the busy world. I was not used to grief, but it still frightened me. I didn't want to leave the presence of those who were still with me, especially my dear Elizabeth, who tried her best to comfort us all. She faced life bravely and took on her responsibilities with courage and enthusiasm. She focused on taking care of her uncle and cousins, whom she loved dearly. During this time, she was more captivating than ever. She used her smiles to brighten our days and put aside her own sorrows to make us feel better.

Finally, the day of my departure came. Clerval spent the last evening with us. He had tried to convince his father to let him come with me and study alongside me, but his father refused. His father was narrow-minded and saw no value in his son's ambitions and desires. Henry was deeply saddened by the fact that he couldn't get a proper education. He didn't say much, but I could see in his eyes and his determined expression that he was resolved to not be bound by the mundane realities of commerce.

52 We stayed up late, unable to part ways or bring ourselves to say the word "Goodbye!" Eventually we went to bed, but with much anticipation. When I was ready to leave, everyone was there. My father, blessing me again, Clerval, giving me a final handshake, Elizabeth, urging me to write frequently, and showing her last gestures of care towards her companion and friend.

53 I climbed into the carriage that would take me away and felt a wave of sadness wash over me. I had always been surrounded by friendly companions, constantly seeking to bring each other joy. But now, I was all alone. Going to the university meant I had to make new friends and learn to take care of myself. My life had always been sheltered and focused on home, so the idea of unfamiliar faces filled me with anxiety. I loved my siblings, Elizabeth, and Clerval; they were like "old familiar faces." But I believed I wasn't ready to be around strangers. These thoughts raced through my mind as I began my journey. But as I traveled, my spirits lifted and my hopes grew. I yearned for knowledge and had often wished I could leave home and experience the world, to be among other people. Now, my desires were being fulfilled, and it would truly be foolish to regret it.

I had plenty of time for these reflections and more during my long and tiring journey to Ingolstadt. Finally, I spotted the tall, white steeple of the town. I got out of the carriage and was shown to my own private room, where I could spend the evening as I pleased.

54 The next day, I delivered my introduction letters and visited

some of the main professors. By chance, or maybe the negative influence that seemed to control me from the moment I left home, I ended up meeting Mr. Krempe, the professor of natural philosophy. He was a strange man, but very knowledgeable in his field. He asked me about my progress in different areas of natural philosophy. I casually mentioned the names of the alchemists I had studied, partly to show my disdain for the subject. The professor was taken aback. "Have you really spent your time studying such nonsense?" he exclaimed.

I confirmed that I had. "Every minute," Mr. Krempe continued, visibly frustrated, "every second you wasted on those books has been completely pointless. You've filled your mind with outdated theories and useless names. Goodness gracious! Where have you been living that no one bothered to inform you that these ideas, which you've eagerly embraced, are a thousand years old and as relevant as ancient history? I never expected to find a follower of Albertus Magnus and Paracelsus in this enlightened and scientific age. My dear sir, you need to start your studies all over again."

With those words, he moved to the side and quickly jotted down a list of books about natural philosophy that he wanted me to get. Then he sent me off, mentioning that he would start a series of lectures on natural philosophy the next week. He also mentioned that M. Waldman, another professor, would give lectures on chemistry on the days he didn't lecture.

I went back home without feeling disappointed because I have already considered those authors to be useless, just like the professor did. However, this encounter with M. Krempe did not make me more interested in pursuing these studies. M. Krempe was a short man with a gruff voice and an unappealing face, which didn't make me like him or his pursuits. In a somewhat philosophical and connected manner, I have explained my past conclusions on these studies. When I was a child, I wasn't satisfied with what the modern natural science professors promised. Due to my young age and lack of guidance in this area, my ideas were confused, and I revisited the knowledge of the past, giving up the discoveries made by recent scientists for the dreams of long-forgotten alchemists. Besides, I had no respect for the practical applications of modern natural philosophy. It used to be different when scientists pursued immortality and power. Even though those aspirations were futile, they were still grand. But now, things had changed. The desire of scientists seemed to be limited to disproving the ideas that had initially sparked my interest in science. I was expected to abandon the lofty visions for realities that held little value.

57   During the first couple of days of my time in Ingolstadt, I spent most of my time getting familiar with the town and meeting the important people who lived there. However, as the following week began, I remembered the information that M. Krempe had given me about the lectures. Even though I wasn't interested in hearing that arrogant man speak from a pulpit, I did remember him mentioning M. Waldman, whom I had never seen before since he was usually out of town.

Out of curiosity and because I had nothing better to do, I decided to go to the lecture hall. M. Waldman entered shortly after, and he was very different from his colleague. He looked to be around fifty years old, but he had a kind and benevolent expression on his face. A few of his temples had grey hair, but the hair at the back of his head was mostly black. He was short but stood tall and had the most pleasant voice I had ever heard. He started his lecture by summarizing the history of chemistry and the advancements made by different scholars, speaking with passion about the most notable discoverers. He then gave a brief overview of the current state of chemistry and explained some of the basic terms. After conducting a few introductory experiments, he concluded by praising modern chemistry, and I will always remember the words he used.

58   "The ancient teachers of this science," he said, "made impossible promises and achieved nothing. The modern masters make much humbler claims. They know that metals cannot be transformed, and the elixir of life is nothing but a fantasy. But these philosophers, who

seem to always have their hands in dirt and their eyes focused on microscopes and crucibles, have indeed performed miracles. They delve into the mysteries of nature and reveal its hidden workings. They explore the heavens, uncover how blood circulates, and understand the nature of the air we breathe. They have acquired incredible powers, allowing them to summon thunderstorms, imitate earthquakes, and even mimic the unseen realm."

Those were the words of the professor, or rather, the words of destiny, spoken to bring about my downfall. As he continued, I felt as if my very soul was engaged in a battle against a tangible adversary. Each key of my being was touched, one by one, activating the mechanisms within me. Chord after chord resounded, and soon my mind was consumed by a single thought, a single idea, a single purpose. The soul of Frankenstein exclaimed, so much has already been accomplished, but I will achieve much more. I will forge a new path, following in the footsteps already laid out. I will explore uncharted powers and unveil the deepest mysteries of creation to the world.

I couldn't sleep that night. My thoughts were in chaos, and I longed for order, but I had no control over it. Eventually, as the morning arrived, I managed to fall asleep. When I woke up, it felt like the thoughts from the previous night were just a dream. All that remained was a determination to return to my old studies and dedicate myself to a science that I believed I had a natural talent for.

On that same day, I visited Mr. Waldman. His demeanor in private was even more gentle and charming than in public. During his lecture, he had carried himself with a certain dignity, but now, in his own home, he was kind and affable. I recounted my previous pursuits to him, much like I had done with his colleague. He listened attentively as I spoke of my studies and smiled when I mentioned the names of Cornelius Agrippa and Paracelsus, but he didn't show the same contempt as Mr. Krempe had.

Mr. Waldman explained that "these men were the ones whose tireless dedication paved the way for modern philosophers to gain their knowledge. They have made it easier for us to give new names and organize the facts they brought to light. The works of genius, no matter how misguided, often end up benefiting humanity in the end."

I paid close attention to his words, which he delivered without any arrogance or pretension. I then admitted that his lecture had changed my negative opinions about modern chemists. I expressed myself respectfully and modestly, like a young student should when speaking to their teacher, without revealing the enthusiasm that fueled my future endeavors. I asked for his advice on which books I should acquire.

"I'm glad," said M. Waldman, "to have found a student like you. If you work hard, I have no doubt you will succeed. Chemistry is an important area of science with a lot of room for improvement. That's why I've dedicated myself to studying it. But I haven't ignored other fields of science either. A person would be a poor chemist if they only focused on that one subject. If you truly want to be a scientist and not just someone who does experiments, I recommend studying all branches of natural philosophy, including math."

Afterwards, he brought me to his lab and showed me the different machines he used. He taught me what equipment I would need and promised to let me use his machines once I had advanced enough in my studies. He also provided me with a list of books that I had asked for. With that, I said goodbye.

This marked a significant day for me; it determined my future path.

CHAPTER

FOUR

 FROM THAT DAY FORWARD, I devoted most of my time to studying natural philosophy, especially chemistry in its broadest sense. I eagerly read the brilliant and insightful works written by modern researchers in these fields. I attended lectures and made connections with the scientists at the university. Even in M. Krempe, despite his unattractive appearance and manners, I discovered a wealth of practical knowledge and valuable information. But it was M. Waldman who became a true friend to me. His kindness was never overshadowed by arrogance, and he taught me with a genuine sincerity and friendly demeanor that kept any trace of arrogance at bay. In countless ways, he made the pursuit of knowledge easier for me, simplifying even the most complex questions and concepts. At first, my dedication wavered and was uncertain, but as I progressed, it grew stronger and more passionate. There were times when morning broke and the stars faded away while I was still engrossed in my laboratory work.

I was completely absorbed in my studies, which led to rapid progress. My dedication amazed my fellow students and impressed my teachers. Professor Krempe would often tease me, asking how my

19

progress compared to that of Cornelius Agrippa. Meanwhile, M. Waldman took great joy in seeing me excel. Two years passed in this manner, during which I didn't visit Geneva. My heart and soul were devoted to making scientific discoveries. The allure of science is hard to understand unless you've experienced it. In other subjects, you can only go as far as those who came before you, but in science, there's always more to discover and be amazed by. By focusing my mind on one particular study, my moderate capacity allowed me to become highly proficient. I was solely devoted to this pursuit, and I improved so rapidly that in two years, I made some notable discoveries in enhancing certain chemical instruments. This gained me respect and admiration at the university. Once I had reached this point, having learned all I could from the professors at Ingolstadt, I realized it was time to return to my friends and hometown. However, an unexpected event prolonged my stay.

63   One of the things that particularly caught my attention was the way the human body is put together, or even any living creature for that matter. I often wondered, where does life come from? It was a daring question, and one that has always been seen as a mystery. But think about how many things we could understand if we just mustered up the courage to ask and investigate. I pondered on these things and decided to focus more on the parts of natural science that deal with how living things work (physiology). If it weren't for my intense passion, studying this subject would have been unbearable and almost impossible. To understand the reasons for life, we must first study death. I learned about the science of anatomy, but that wasn't enough. I also needed to observe how bodies naturally decay and decompose. My father had taught me to never be afraid of supernatural stories or believe in ghosts. Darkness didn't frighten me, and a graveyard was simply a place where lifeless bodies lay, no longer beautiful or strong, consumed by worms. But now, I had to face the cause and progression of this decay, and spend days and nights in vaults and burial grounds. Every detail became unbearable to my sensitive human emotions. I witnessed how a once perfect

human form degraded and wasted away. I saw the ugliness of death replacing the lively glow of life. I saw how the wonders of the human eye and brain were inherited by worms. I paused, carefully examining and analyzing every little detail that led from life to death, and from death to life. And then, in the midst of that darkness, a sudden burst of light illuminated everything—it was a light so brilliant and wondrous, yet so simple. As I marveled at the immense possibilities that it revealed, I couldn't help but be surprised that, among all the brilliant minds who had studied the same science, I alone had stumbled upon such an astonishing secret.

Remember, what I am about to share is not the ramblings of a crazy person. I am as certain of this truth as the sun is certain to shine in the sky. Although it may seem miraculous, the process of discovery I went through was clear and reasonable. After days and nights of exhausting work, I finally figured out how life and creation come about. What's more, I gained the ability to give life to inanimate objects.

The initial shock I felt upon this revelation quickly turned into joy and ecstasy. After investing so much time and effort into this endeavor, achieving my ultimate goal all at once was incredibly fulfilling. However, this discovery was so significant and overwhelming that it wiped away all the steps that led me to it, leaving only the final outcome in my view. This knowledge had been the pursuit and longing of the wisest individuals since the beginning of time, and now it was right within my reach. But it didn't unravel before me like a magical scene. Instead, the information I had acquired guided me to direct my efforts toward the object of my search, rather than immediately presenting it. It was like I was an Arabian who had been buried among the deceased but had discovered a way back to life, with only a faint and seemingly insignificant light to guide me.

I can tell from your excitement and curious gaze, my friend, that you're hoping to learn the secret I hold. However, I cannot reveal it to you just yet. Please be patient and hear my entire story, and you will understand why I am being cautious. I will not lead you astray, like I was led in the past when I was eager and unaware of the consequences. I want to spare you from destruction and inevitable despair. Take heed from my experience, if not from my advice, and understand the dangers of seeking knowledge. There is much more happiness in believing that one's hometown is the whole world, than in striving to surpass the limits of one's own nature.

66   When I discovered such an amazing power in my possession, I spent a long time considering how to use it. Even though I could give life to a body, creating a complex and detailed frame with all its fibers, muscles, and veins was incredibly difficult. At first, I was unsure whether I should create a being like myself or something simpler. However, my initial success filled me with so much confidence that I believed I could bring to life an animal as intricate and remarkable as a human. The materials I had at my disposal didn't seem sufficient for such a challenging task, but I never doubted that I would ultimately succeed. I prepared myself for many setbacks. For instance, my experiments could continuously fail, and in the end, my creation could be flawed. However, as I considered the constant progress in science and technology, I found hope that my current efforts would lay the groundwork for future success. I didn't see the vastness and complexity of my plan as evidence of its impossibility. With these thoughts in mind, I began the process of creating a human being. The smallness of the parts I had to work with made the task slower than anticipated, so I decided to go against my initial plan and make the being rather huge, standing about eight feet tall and proportionally large. Once I made this decision and spent several months successfully collecting and organizing my materials, I finally started my project.

67   No one can understand the many feelings which pushed me forward. Life and death appeared to me ideal bounds, which I should break through, and then cast light into our dark world. A new species would bless me as its creator and source. Many happy and excellent natures would owe their being to me. No father could claim the grat-

itude of his child so completely as I should deserve theirs. Pursuing these reflections, I thought, that if I could bestow life upon lifeless matter, I might in process of time be able to renew life where death had already taken it.

68   These thoughts kept my spirits up as I pursued my work with unwavering passion. My face became pale from studying and my body grew thin from being confined. Sometimes, when I was so close to success, I would fail, but I continued to hold onto the hope that the next day or the next hour would bring. I had a secret hope that only I knew, to which I had dedicated myself. I worked fervently, staying up late into the night, with a relentless eagerness, searching every corner of nature for answers. The horrors of my secret experiments are unimaginable as I tampered with the dampness of the grave and tortured animals in order to bring life to inanimate matter. My limbs now tremble and my eyes swim with the memories, but at that time, an uncontrollable and almost frantic impulse pushed me forward. I felt as though I had lost all sense of self except for this single pursuit. It was only a temporary trance that made me feel more intensely, but once the unnatural drive subsided, I returned to my normal routine. I collected bones from graveyards and dissected the human body with impure hands. In a lonely room at the top of the house, separated from the rest by a hallway and stairs, I kept my workshop of grotesque creation. My eyes bulged from their sockets as I worked on the smallest details. The dissecting room and the slaughterhouse provided many of the materials I needed. Often, I would be repulsed by my own actions, but my eagerness pushed me forward, intensifying with each passing day, bringing me closer and closer to completing my work.

69   I spent the summer months completely consumed by one single pursuit. It was during the most beautiful season. However, I was oblivious to the beauty of nature. The same emotions that caused me to neglect my surroundings also caused me to forget about my friends who were miles away and whom I hadn't seen in a long time. I knew that my silence worried them, and I couldn't forget the words

of my father: "I understand that as long as you are content with yourself, you will think of us with affection and we will hear from you regularly. You must forgive me if I interpret any break in our correspondence as a sign that you have neglected your other responsibilities."

I was well aware of my father's sentiments, but I couldn't pry my thoughts away from my work. It was revolting in nature, yet it held an irresistible grip on my imagination. I wanted to delay anything related to my feelings of affection until I had completed the all-consuming task that had overtaken every aspect of my being.

70 I thought at the time that my father would be unfair if he blamed me for neglecting my duties, but now I understand why he might have had some valid concerns. A person should always strive to have a calm and peaceful mind, and not let their emotions or fleeting desires disrupt their inner peace. I don't believe that the pursuit of knowledge is exempt from this principle. If the study you are dedicated to has the potential to weaken your emotions and destroy your enjoyment of simple, pure pleasures, then that study is certainly not appropriate for the human mind. If everyone followed this principle and didn't allow any pursuit to interfere with their family life, Greece would not have been enslaved, Caesar would not have harmed his country, America's discovery would have been more gradual, and the empires of Mexico and Peru would not have fallen.

But I am getting sidetracked and moralizing during the most exciting part of my story. I can see by your expressions that you want me to continue.

71 My father didn't scold me in his letters, but he did ask more questions about what I was doing. I spent the whole winter, spring, and summer working, but I didn't have time to appreciate the beauty of nature like I used to. I was completely consumed by my work. By the time I finished, the leaves had already fallen and I realized how successful I had been. But my excitement was overshadowed by anxiety. I felt like a slave working tirelessly in unhealthy conditions, rather than an artist enjoying my favorite activity. Every night, I was

plagued by a slow fever and my nerves were on edge. The smallest noise or movement startled me, and I avoided people as if I had done something wrong. I started to worry about the toll my obsession had taken on me. I kept going thanks to my determination, believing that once my creation was done, I could recover my health through exercise and leisure.

CHAPTER
FIVE

⁷² On a dark, gloomy night in November, I finally witnessed the completion of my experiments. Filled with anxiety and nearly consumed by my desire, I gathered the tools of my work around me. My goal was to bring life to the inanimate creature that lay before me. The clock struck one in the morning, rain drumming against the windows, and my flickering candle was on the verge of extinguishing. In the fading light, I saw the creature's dull yellow eye open, its breathing shallow and its limbs trembling uncontrollably.

Words fail to capture the overwhelming emotions I experienced at this catastrophic moment. How can I describe the horror of the being I had strived so painstakingly to create? Its limbs were proportionate and its features carefully chosen for their beauty. But beauty? Oh God! Its yellow skin barely concealed the pulsating muscles and veins beneath. Its hair, jet-black and flowing, contrasted grotesquely against its watery eyes, almost the same color as the pale sockets in which they were set. Its complexion was withered and its lips straight and dark.

⁷³ The ups and downs of life are not as unpredictable as the emotions we experience as humans. I had worked diligently for

almost two years, with the sole purpose of bringing a lifeless body to life. In this pursuit, I sacrificed my rest and my health. My desire to succeed went beyond reasonable limits. But now that I had finished, the enchanting dream disappeared, leaving me with only horror and revulsion. I couldn't bear to look at the creature I had created, so I hurriedly left the room. I wandered around my bedroom for a long time, unable to find peace and sleep. Eventually, exhaustion overcame the earlier turmoil, and I threw myself onto the bed, still fully dressed, hoping for a few moments of forgetfulness. However, it was in vain. I did fall asleep, but my dreams were filled with madness. I imagined seeing Elizabeth, radiant and healthy, walking in the streets of Ingolstadt. Overjoyed and surprised, I embraced her, but as I kissed her lips, they turned ashen, resembling death. Her appearance changed, and I believed I was holding the lifeless body of my deceased mother. She was covered in a burial shroud, and I witnessed worms wriggling in the fabric. I jolted awake in horror, my forehead covered in cold sweat, my teeth chattering, and every muscle convulsing. In the dim, yellow moonlight that peeked through the closed shutters, I saw the wretched creature - the miserable monster I had brought to life. He held back the curtains of the bed, and his eyes, if one could call them that, were fixed on me. His jaws opened, and he uttered incomprehensible sounds, while a twisted smile appeared on his cheeks. Perhaps he was trying to communicate, but I couldn't hear anything. One of his hands stretched out, seemingly to hold me back, but I managed to escape and hurried downstairs. I sought refuge in the courtyard of the house I lived in, where I spent the rest of the night anxiously pacing back and forth, alert to every sound, fearing that it would announce the arrival of the demonic corpse I had, wretchedly, given life to.

Oh, the face of that creature was truly horrifying! It was more terrifying than a mummy brought back to life. Even Dante himself could not have imagined such a hideous sight.

I had a terrible night. My heart raced so fast and strongly that I could feel the pounding in every vein. At other times, I felt so weak and worn out that I could barely stay standing. Along with this terror, I also felt a deep sense of disappointment. The dreams that had brought me joy and tranquility for so long had now turned into a nightmare. It happened so suddenly, and the change was so complete.

Finally, the morning arrived with its gloomy and rainy weather. I could see the church of Ingolstadt with its white steeple and clock, indicating that it was six o'clock. The gatekeeper opened the court-yard gate, which had been my refuge for the night, and I stepped out onto the streets. I walked quickly, as if trying to avoid the creature that I feared would appear at every corner. I didn't dare return to my room, instead feeling compelled to keep moving, even though I was soaked by the rain coming from the bleak and unwelcoming sky.

75 I walked around aimlessly for a while, trying to distract myself from the heavy burden on my mind. The streets seemed unfamiliar, and I couldn't focus on where I was or what I was doing. My heart was racing with fear, and I hurried along, unable to look around me:

"Like someone walking alone on a deserted road,

Feeling fear and dread in their soul,

And once they turn around, they keep walking,

Never daring to look back,

Because they know a horrifying monster

Is lurking just behind."

I kept going until I reached the inn where the coaches usually stopped. I paused there for no apparent reason and stared at a coach approaching me from the other end of the street. As it got closer, I realized it was the Swiss coach. It stopped right where I was stand-ing, and when the door opened, I saw Henry Clerval inside. He immediately jumped out when he saw me. "My dear Frankenstein," he exclaimed, "how happy I am to see you! It's so lucky you're here just as I'm getting off!"

76 I was overjoyed to see Clerval. His presence reminded me of my father, Elizabeth, and all the cherished memories of home. I held his hand tightly, instantly forgetting my horror and misfortune; for the

first time in months, I felt a sense of calm and pure joy. I warmly welcomed my friend and we headed towards my college. Clerval talked about our friends and his own good luck in being allowed to come to Ingolstadt. He said, "You can imagine how difficult it was for me to convince my father that knowledge extends beyond just book-keeping. At first, he didn't believe me, always giving me the same response as the Dutch schoolmaster in the Vicar of Wakefield: 'I can have a comfortable life without Greek, eating well without Greek.' Eventually, his love for me triumphed over his aversion to learning, and he gave me permission to embark on a journey of discovery to expand my knowledge."

"I am absolutely delighted to see you, but please tell me how my father, brothers, and Elizabeth are doing."

"They're doing well and are happy, although they worry a bit because they don't hear from you very often. By the way, I want to talk to you about them a little myself. But hey, my dear Franken-stein," he added, pausing and looking straight at my face, "I didn't notice before how sickly you look; so thin and pale. You appear as if you've been staying up for many nights."

"You're right, I've been really busy with something lately that I haven't gotten enough rest, as you can see. But I hope, sincerely hope, that all of these tasks are finally finished and that I'm free now."

I was shaking a lot; I couldn't stand the thought of, and even less talk about, what happened last night. I walked quickly, and we soon got to my college. Then it hit me, and it made me shudder, that the creature I had left in my room might still be there, alive, and moving around. I dreaded seeing this monster, but I was even more afraid of Henry seeing him. So, I begged him to wait at the bottom of the stairs for a few minutes while I rushed up to my own room. I had my hand on the doorknob before I remembered myself. I stopped then, and a cold shiver ran through me. I forcefully flung the door open, like how children do when they expect a ghost to be waiting for them on the other side, but there was nothing there. I cautiously walked inside:

the room was empty; and my bedroom was also free from its horrifying guest. I could hardly believe that such a stroke of luck had happened to me; but when I finally realized that my enemy had indeed run away, I clapped my hands with joy and hurried downstairs to Clerval.

79 We went up to my room, and the servant soon brought breakfast. But I couldn't control myself. It wasn't just joy that overwhelmed me; my body felt overly sensitive, and my heartbeat raced. I couldn't stay still for even a moment. I jumped over the chairs, clapped my hands, and burst out laughing. At first, Clerval thought my unusual behavior was due to happiness over his arrival. However, as he looked at me more closely, he saw a craziness in my eyes that he couldn't understand. My loud, unrestrained, heartless laughter frightened and amazed him.

"My dear Victor," he cried, "what in God's name is wrong? Don't laugh like that. You look so ill. What's causing all of this?"

"Don't ask me," I cried, covering my eyes with my hands, because I thought I saw the dreaded ghost appear in the room. "He can tell you. Oh, save me, save me!" I imagined that the monster was grabbing me. I fought desperately and fell into a fainting spell.

Poor Clerval! How must he have felt? The meeting he had been so excited about had suddenly turned into bitterness. But I didn't witness his sorrow, because I was unconscious and didn't regain my senses for a very long time.

80 This was the start of a nervous fever that kept me confined for several months. Throughout that entire time, Henry was the only one who took care of me. Later on, I found out that he didn't want my father, who was old and not well-suited for long journeys, and my sister Elizabeth, who would have been devastated by my illness, to suffer any more grief. So he hid from them just how sick I was. He knew that he would be the best and most caring nurse for me, and he firmly believed that by taking care of me, he was doing the kindest thing he could for them.

But the truth was, I was really sick. Only with the immense and constant care from my friend was I able to recover. The image of the monster I had created haunted me constantly, and I couldn't stop raving about him. Henry must have been surprised by my words at first, thinking it was all nonsensical ramblings from my troubled mind. But the fact that I kept bringing up the same topic over and over again made him believe that my illness was truly caused by something extraordinary and terrible.

Slowly, and with many setbacks that worried and saddened my friend, I recovered. I remember the first time I was able to enjoy seeing the world around me again. I noticed that the fallen leaves had disappeared and that new buds were growing on the trees outside my window. It was a beautiful spring, and the season played a big role in my healing. Gradually, feelings of joy and love returned to me. My sadness faded away, and soon I was as cheerful as I was before I fell ill.

"Oh, dear Clerval," I exclaimed, "you have been so kind and good to me. Instead of spending the winter studying, as you planned, you have been by my side in my sick room. How can I ever repay you? I feel so guilty for causing you this disappointment, but I hope you can forgive me."

"You will repay me completely if you don't worry yourself and focus on getting better as quickly as possible. Since you seem to be in good spirits, may I talk to you about something?" Clerval asked.

I felt a tremor of anxiety. What could he be referring to? Was he hinting at something I couldn't even allow myself to think about?

"Take a moment to calm yourself," said Clerval, noticing the change in my complexion. "If it upsets you, I won't bring it up. But your father and cousin would be overjoyed to receive a letter from you written in your own hand. They don't really know how sick you've been, and they're worried about your long silence."

"Is that it, Henry? Did you really think that I wouldn't immediately think of my friends who deserve my love so much?"

"If you're feeling like this now, my friend, you might be pleased to know that there's a letter here for you that has been waiting for a few days. It's from your cousin, I think."

CHAPTER
SIX

 CLERVAL THEN HANDED me the letter. It came from my cousin Elizabeth:

"Dearest Cousin,

You have been very sick, and even though Henry's letters have been kind and reassuring, they are not enough to calm my worries for you. You are not allowed to write or even hold a pen, but I need just a few words from you, Victor, to ease our anxieties. I have been hoping with each mail delivery that I would receive a message from you, and because of my insistence, my uncle has refrained from making a trip to Ingolstadt. I have wished many times that I could go myself and take care of you, rather than leaving it to some paid nurse who could never understand your needs or care for you like your own cousin. But that is in the past now: Clerval tells me that you are indeed improving. I anxiously await your own handwritten confirmation of this news."

 "Get well soon and come back to us. You will find a happy and loving home, with friends who care deeply about you. Your father is healthy and just wants to see you, to know that you are well. He will always have a kind and caring expression on his face, without a

33

worry in the world. You would be so pleased to see how much our younger brother Ernest has improved! He is now sixteen years old and full of energy and enthusiasm. He dreams of becoming a true Swiss and serving in the military abroad, but we can't bear to let him go until his older brother returns. Our uncle doesn't approve of the idea of a career in a distant country, but Ernest doesn't have your dedication to academics. He sees studying as a burden; instead, he prefers spending his time outdoors, climbing hills and rowing on the lake. I'm afraid he may become idle if we don't give in and allow him to pursue the profession he has chosen."

85 Not much has changed since you left us, except for our children growing up. The serene lake and majestic mountains have remained the same, and our peaceful home and contented hearts abide by steady principles. I find comfort and amusement in my simple daily tasks. I am surrounded by only joyful and kind faces. There has been only one significant change in our small household since you departed. Do you recall when Justine Moritz became a part of our family? You probably do not, so let me briefly tell you her story. Justine was the third child of Madame Moritz, a widow with four children. Strangely, her mother could not bear Justine, despite being her father's favorite, and treated her poorly after his passing. My aunt noticed this mistreatment, and when Justine turned twelve, she convinced her mother to let her live with us. The democratic values of our nation have fostered a society with simpler and happier customs compared to the influential monarchies that surround us. As a result, there is less distinction between social classes, and even the lower classes are not as impoverished or disregarded, leading to more refined and moral behavior. In Geneva, being a servant does not have the same connotations as it does in France and England. When Justine joined our family, she learned the responsibilities of a servant, an occupation in our fortunate country that does not imply ignorance or the sacrifice of one's human dignity.

86 Dear Justine, you might remember that you were highly regarded by my dear aunt. I recall you once mentioned how a single look from

Justine could make anyone feel better. She has a genuine and joyful countenance. My aunt grew to love her tremendously, and as a result, she decided to provide Justine with a higher education than originally planned. This kindness was gratefully repaid; Justine was the most appreciative person one could ever meet. I don't mean that she made any elaborate declarations– I never heard her utter one– but her eyes alone revealed her adoration. Although Justine had a cheerful disposition that sometimes led her to act without thinking, she paid great attention to every move my aunt made. Justine saw her as the epitome of excellence and strived to imitate her mannerisms and way of speaking. To this day, Justine often reminds me of my aunt.

When my dearest aunt passed away, everyone became so filled with sorrow that they failed to notice poor Justine, who had been devotedly caring for her during her illness. Justine herself fell ill, but there were more trials awaiting her.

In time, one by one, her brothers and sister passed away, leaving her mother alone, except for her neglected daughter. The woman's conscience was troubled, believing that the deaths were a punishment from heaven for her favoritism. Being a Roman Catholic, her confessor likely reinforced this idea. A few months after you left for Ingolstadt, Justine was summoned home by her remorseful mother. It was a heartbreaking farewell as she left our house. The loss of my aunt had changed her greatly; grief had softened her vibrant personality, replacing it with a gentle and kind demeanor. However, her return to her mother's home did not bring her joy. Her mother's repentance was unstable, sometimes begging for forgiveness, but more often blaming Justine for the deaths of her siblings. The constant emotional torment eventually caused Madame Moritz to decline, initially increasing her irritability before finding eternal peace with her passing in the early days of winter. Justine has since come back to us, and I can assure you, my dear friend, that I hold a deep love for her. She is intelligent, gentle, and exquisitely beautiful.

As I mentioned before, her presence and mannerisms constantly remind me of my beloved aunt.

88   I want to share some updates with you, my dear cousin, about young William. He has grown so much and looks adorable with his big, sparkling blue eyes, long dark lashes, and curly hair. When he smiles, he has cute little dimples on his rosy cheeks. He's already had a couple of crushes, but his favorite is a pretty girl named Louisa, who is five years old.

Now, dear Victor, I know you're curious about what's happening in Geneva. The lovely Miss Mansfield has been getting congratulations on her upcoming marriage to an Englishman named John Melbourne. Her not-so-attractive sister, Manon, got married to a wealthy banker named M. Duvillard last autumn. Your friend from school, Louis Manoir, has had some tough times since Clerval left Geneva. But he's starting to feel better and there are rumors about him marrying a lively and pretty French lady named Madame Tavernier. She's older than Manoir, but everyone seems to really like her.

Writing this letter has cheered me up, my dear cousin. However, my worries come back as I finish. Please write back to us, even if it's just one line or one word. We would be so grateful. A big thank you to Henry for his kindness, affection, and the many letters he has sent. We truly appreciate it. Goodbye, dear cousin. Take care of yourself and please, I beg you, write back!

With love,

Elizabeth Lavenza.

89   "Geneva, March 18th, 17—."

"Oh Elizabeth! I said excitedly after reading her letter, "I'll write right away to ease their worries." I wrote the letter, even though it exhausted me greatly. But I was getting better, and in two weeks I was able to leave my room.

After my recovery, one of the first things I had to do was introduce Clerval to the professors at the university. Unfortunately, during this process, I experienced rough treatment that was not suitable for my wounded mind. Ever since that dreadful night, when my work ended and my misfortune began, I had developed a strong dislike for the subject of natural philosophy. Even when I was fully healed, just seeing a chemical instrument would bring back all the pain of my nervous symptoms. Henry noticed this and made sure to keep all my equipment out of sight. He even changed my room because he could tell I had grown to dislike the one that used to be my laboratory. But all of Clerval's efforts were in vain when I visited the professors. Professor Waldman unintentionally inflicted torment on me when he kindly and warmly praised the incredible progress I had made in the sciences. He quickly realized I had a distaste for the subject, but he didn't know the true reason behind my feelings. He thought it was just modesty and shifted the conversation from my improvement to the science itself, hoping to engage me. What could I do? He meant well, but he only caused me more anguish. It felt as if he carefully placed all those instruments in front of me, the very ones that would be used to slowly and cruelly end my life. I struggled internally, but I couldn't show him how much pain I was in. Clerval, always perceptive of others' emotions, decided to change the subject since he could tell it was making me uncomfortable. He claimed ignorance as an excuse. The conversation then took a more general direction. I was grateful to my friend, though I didn't say it out loud. I could see that he was surprised, but he never pushed me to reveal my secret. Even though I loved him deeply and respected him endlessly, I could never bring myself to confide in him about the event that haunted my thoughts. I feared that sharing the details with someone else would only make it more deeply ingrained in my memory.

Mr. Krempe was not as cooperative, and in my state of extreme sensitivity, his harsh and blunt praise caused me even more distress than the kind approval of Mr. Waldman. "Oh, the fellow!" he exclaimed. "M. Clerval, I assure you, he has surpassed all of us. Yes, go ahead and stare, but it is still true. A young man who, just a few years ago, believed in Cornelius Agrippa as strongly as he believed in the gospel, has now risen to the top of the university. And if he doesn't get knocked down soon, we will all be embarrassed. Yes, yes," he continued, noticing the pain on my face, "Mr. Frankenstein is modest, an excellent quality in a young man. Young men should doubt themselves, you see, M. Clerval. I myself was like that when I was young, but it doesn't last very long."

Mr. Krempe had now begun to praise himself, which fortunately changed the topic from something that bothered me so much.

92   My friend Clerval and I had different interests when it came to academics. While I was engrossed in natural science, Clerval was passionate about studying the oriental languages. He saw it as a way to pursue a fulfilling and adventurous life. Excited by his aspirations, I joined him in studying Persian, Arabic, and Sanskrit. I found solace in these new pursuits, as they provided a welcome distraction from my own struggles and allowed me to bond with Clerval. Although I didn't delve into the languages as deeply as he did, I still found value in understanding their meaning. The works of the orientalists brought me both knowledge and comfort. Their writings had a unique power to soothe my soul and uplift my spirits, something I hadn't experienced with other literature from Greece and Rome. In their stories, life seemed to revolve around a vibrant sun, fragrant gardens, complicated relationships, and intense emotions. It was a stark contrast to the more stoic poetry of ancient times.

93   During the summer, I kept myself busy with these activities. I had planned to return to Geneva in the fall, but my journey was delayed until the following spring when the roads became impassable with snow. I felt frustrated by the delay because I was eager to see my hometown and my dear friends. I had stayed longer than intended because I didn't want to leave Clerval behind in an unfamiliar place before he had a chance to get to know anyone there.

Despite the delay, we managed to have a pleasant winter, and when spring finally arrived, its beauty made up for the long wait.

It was already May, and I was expecting a letter any day now to determine the date of my departure. However, Henry suggested that we take a walking tour around Ingolstadt to say goodbye to the country. I happily agreed to this idea. Plus, Clerval had always been my favorite companion on these types of outings in my home country.

We spent two weeks on these walks: my health and spirits had already improved, and they became even stronger thanks to the fresh air, the natural sights we encountered, and my friend's company. In the past, my studies had isolated me from other people and made me unsociable, but Clerval brought out the best in me. He reminded me how to appreciate nature and the joyful faces of children. You were truly an excellent friend! You loved me sincerely and tried to raise my spirits to match your own. My selfish pursuits had confined and limited me, but your kindness and affection revived my senses and made me the happy person I used to be a few years ago, loved and beloved by all, without any sorrow or worry. When I was happy, the beauty of the natural world had the power to give me the most delightful feelings. A clear sky and green fields filled me with pure joy. The current season was truly divine; spring flowers blossomed on the hedges, while the flowers of summer were beginning to bud. I was finally free from the thoughts that had weighed me down the previous year, no matter how hard I tried to shake them off.

Henry was happy to see me so cheerful, and he sincerely understood and shared my emotions. He made an effort to entertain me, while also expressing his own deep feelings. I was amazed by his creative thinking during this time. His conversations were full of imagination. He told great stories and held conversation that was interesting.

We returned to our school on a Sunday afternoon. The villagers were dancing, and everyone we encountered seemed joyful and content. My own mood was elevated, and I skipped along with a sense of pure joy and happiness.

CHAPTER

SEVEN

UPON MY RETURN, I discovered a letter from my father:

"Dear Victor,

You have likely been eagerly awaiting a letter to inform you of the date you should come back home. At first, I considered writing just a few lines, simply stating the day I expected you. However, that would be an unkind act, and I cannot bring myself to do it. My son, imagine your surprise, expecting a joyful and warm welcome, only to be met with tears and misery instead. How can I share our misfortune with you, Victor? Surely, your time away has not made you immune to our happiness and sorrows. How can I cause pain to my son who has been gone for so long? I wish I could prepare you for the terrible news, but I know it is impossible. Even now, your eyes quickly scan the words on this page, searching for the ones that will bring you the horrifying tidings.

"William is dead! Our sweet child, who always brought smiles to my face and warmed my heart, who was so kind yet full of joy! Victor, he has been murdered!

"I won't attempt to console you; instead, I will simply explain what happened."

41

"Last Thursday, May 7th, I, my niece, and your two brothers went for a walk in Plainpalais. The weather was warm and peaceful, so we decided to walk a bit further than usual. By the time we thought about heading back, it was already getting dark, and we couldn't find William and Ernest, who had gone ahead of us. We waited on a bench, hoping they would return soon. Eventually, Ernest came back and asked if we had seen his brother. He explained that they had been playing together when William ran off to hide, and despite searching for him for a long time, he never came back.

This news worried us, and we continued searching until nightfall. Elizabeth surmised that William might have made his way back home, but he wasn't there. Determined to find him, we returned with torches. I couldn't rest knowing that my beloved son was lost and vulnerable in the damp and dark night, and Elizabeth was tormented with anguish. At around five in the morning, I stumbled upon my precious boy. The previous day, he had been vibrant and full of life, but now he lay motionless and pale on the grass, with the telltale mark of the murderer's hand on his neck.

"He was taken back to our house, and the sorrow on my face revealed the truth to Elizabeth. She was very eager to see his body. At first, I tried to stop her, but she insisted. She entered the room where he lay and quickly examined his neck. Then, she clasped her hands and cried out, 'Oh God! I have killed my beloved child!'

"She fainted and it was very hard to revive her. When she finally woke up, all she could do was cry and sigh. She told me that on that same evening, William had begged her to let him wear a valuable picture of your mother that she had. The picture is gone now, and it was probably the reason why the murderer did what he did. We currently have no idea where he is, even though we are doing everything we can to find him. But finding him won't bring back my dear William!

"Please, my dearest Victor, you are the only one who can comfort Elizabeth. She cries non-stop and blames herself unfairly for his death. Her words hurt me deeply. We are all miserable, but won't that be even more of a reason for you, my son, to come back and be our source of comfort? Your dear mother! Oh Victor, I am grateful that she didn't have to see the awful, tragic death of her youngest child!"

"Come, Victor; not dwelling on thoughts of revenge against the murderer, but with feelings of peace and kindness that will heal instead of worsening the wounds of our hearts. Enter the house of sorrow, my friend, but with love and care for those who care about you, and not with hatred for your enemies.

"Your loving and troubled father,

"Alphonse Frankenstein.

"Geneva, May 12th, 17—."

CLERVAL, who had watched my face as I read this letter, was surprised to see the despair that replaced the initial joy I felt upon receiving news from my friends. I placed the letter on the table and covered my face with my hands.

"My dear Frankenstein," Henry exclaimed, seeing me weep bitterly, "will you always be unhappy? My dear friend, what happened?"

I motioned for him to pick up the letter while I paced back and forth in great agitation. Tears also welled up in Clerval's eyes as he read the account of my misfortune.

"I cannot console you, my friend," he said. "Your tragedy is irreparable. What do you plan to do?"

"To go to Geneva immediately: come with me, Henry, so we can arrange for the horses."

During our walk, Clerval tried to offer some comforting words, although he could only express his deep sympathy. "Poor William!" he said. "Such a dear and lovely child, now sleeping with his angelic mother! Anyone who had seen him shining and happy in his youthful beauty couldn't help but weep over his untimely loss. To die in such a terrible way, to feel the murderer's hands! How much more of a monster, someone who could destroy such a radiant innocence! Poor little boy! We have only one consolation; his friends mourn and weep, but he is now at peace. The pain is over, his suffering has ended forever. He lies beneath the ground, free from any pain. He can no longer be pitied; that is reserved for those who survive him."

Clerval spoke these words as we hurried through the streets. They left a lasting impression on my mind, and I remembered them later when I was alone. But as soon as the horses arrived, I hastily got into a carriage and bid farewell to my friend.

101   As I journeyed, I felt very sad. Initially, I wanted to rush on to comfort and empathize with my loved ones who were grieving. However, as I neared my hometown, I started to slow down. The multitude of emotions overwhelmed me. I passed through familiar scenes from my youth that I hadn't seen in almost six years. I couldn't help but wonder how everything might have changed during that time. One sudden and devastating change had already occurred, but there could have been a thousand other small circumstances that gradually brought about other alterations. They may have been done more quietly, but no less significant. Fear overcame me, and I couldn't bring myself to move forward. I was afraid of countless unknown evils that made me tremble, even though I couldn't quite pinpoint them.

I stayed in Lausanne for two days, feeling this painful state of mind. I looked out at the calm lake, its waters still and serene. Everything around it was peaceful, and the snowy mountains, often described as "the palaces of nature," remained unchanged. Gradually, the tranquility of the heavenly scene restored me, and I continued my journey towards Geneva.

The road followed along the lake, which became narrower as I got closer to my hometown. I could see the dark sides of Jura and the bright peak of Mont Blanc more clearly. I couldn't help but weep, like a child. "Dear mountains! My beautiful lake! How do you welcome this wanderer? Your peaks are clear, and the sky and lake are calm and blue. Does this signal peace or mock my unhappiness?"

I'm afraid that I may become boring if I spend too much time on these initial details, but during that time I was happy. My homeland, my cherished homeland! Only a native can truly understand how joyful I was to see your rivers, your mountains, and, most of all, your beautiful lake once more!

However, as I got closer to home, sadness and fear took hold of me once again. The darkness of night surrounded me, and with the mountains barely visible, my mood became even gloomier. The scene appeared vast and filled with darkness, and I vaguely sensed that I was meant to become the most miserable person in the world. Alas! I predicted correctly, but I was mistaken in one aspect: I couldn't even conceive a small fraction of the suffering I was destined to endure.

When I arrived near Geneva, it was already dark and the town gates were closed. I had to spend the night in a village called Secheron, which was about half a mile away from the city. The sky was clear and since I couldn't sleep, I decided to go to the place where my dear William was murdered. Since I couldn't go through the town, I had to take a boat across the lake to get to Plainpalais. During this short boat ride, I saw beautiful lightning dancing on top of Mont Blanc. The storm seemed to be approaching quickly, so when I reached land, I climbed a small hill to watch it. The storm moved closer, the sky got cloudy, and soon I felt the rain starting to fall in large drops, but it quickly became more intense.

I left my seat and continued walking, even though it was getting darker and the storm was getting stronger. The thunder crashed loudly above me, echoing from Salêve, the Jura Mountains, and the Alps of Savoy. I could see dazzling flashes of lightning that illuminated the lake, making it look like a vast sheet of fire. Then, everything would suddenly become very dark until my eyes adjusted from the previous flash. The storm, as often happens in Switzerland, appeared in different parts of the sky at the same time. The most intense part of the storm was directly north of the town, over the area of the lake between Belrive promontory and the village of Copêt. Another part of the storm lit up Jura with faint flashes, while another part made the Môle, a pointed mountain to the east of the lake, sometimes visible and sometimes hidden.

105   As I watched the powerful storm, both beautiful and terrifying, I continued walking quickly. The intense battle in the sky lifted my spirits, and I couldn't help but exclaim, "William, my dear angel! This is your funeral, your solemn tribute!" As I spoke these words, I noticed in the darkness a figure emerging from behind a group of trees nearby. I stood motionless, staring intently, knowing that I couldn't be mistaken. A flash of lightning illuminated the object, revealing its form to me: a towering and horribly deformed creature, more monstrous than any human could be. Instantly, I realized that it was the creature, the hideous monster that I had brought to life. What was it doing there? Could it be (the mere thought sent shivers down my spine) the murderer of my brother? The idea crossed my mind and with it came an unshakable certainty. My teeth began to chatter, and I had to lean against a tree for support. The figure swiftly passed by me and disappeared into the darkness. No human being could have harmed that innocent child. He was the murderer! I could not deny it. The presence of that thought alone was undeniable proof. I considered chasing after the devil, but it would have been pointless, for another flash revealed him hanging among the rocks on the almost perpendicular slope of Mont Salêve, a hill that borders Plainpalais to the south. He quickly reached the summit and vanished from sight.

106   I stood there without moving. The loud thunder finally stopped, but the rain kept pouring down, making everything dark and impossible to see. I couldn't help but think about all the things I had been trying to forget: the whole process of creating this creature, the shock of seeing it come alive in my own room, and then its sudden disappearance. It had been almost two years since that night when it first came to life, and now I had to ask myself, was this its first act of

violence? Oh, how terrible it was to realize that I had unleashed a monster into the world, a monster who found joy in causing pain and suffering. And now, had it taken the life of my own brother?

No one can understand the immense pain I felt for the rest of that night. I was left outside in the cold and wet, but I barely noticed the discomfort. My mind was consumed with thoughts of darkness and despair. I saw this creature, whom I had created and given the ability to carry out acts of horror like the one it had just committed, as if it were my own vampire, my own tormented spirit set free from the grave, forced to destroy everything that was dear to me.

The day began, and I walked towards the town. The gates were open, and I hurried to my father's house. My first intention was to find out what I knew about the killer and immediately start a search. However, I hesitated when I thought about the story I had to tell. A being that I myself had created and given life to had encountered me at midnight in the dangerous mountains. I also remembered the nervous fever I had suffered from when I first brought the creature to life, which would make my tale seem like the delusions of someone who is mentally unwell. I knew that if someone else had told me such a story, I would have dismissed it as the ramblings of a mad person. Moreover, the unique abilities of the creature would make it impossible to track down, even if my family believed me enough to begin a search. And even if we did try to pursue it, what good would it do? Who could catch a creature capable of climbing the steep slopes of Mont Salêve? These thoughts made up my mind, and I decided to stay quiet.

It was around five o'clock in the morning when I entered my father's house. I instructed the servants not to disturb the family and went to the library to wait for their usual waking hour.

Six years had passed, like a fleeting dream, with only one unforgettable memory. I stood in the very same spot where I had last hugged my father before leaving for Ingolstadt. My beloved and respected parent was still with me. I looked at the painting of my mother, displayed above the fireplace. It depicted Caroline Beaufort in a state of despair, kneeling beside her deceased father's coffin. She wore simple clothes and had a pale complexion, although there was an undeniable aura of grace and beauty that made it hard to feel sorry for her. Below this painting was a small portrait of William, and tears welled in my eyes as I gazed upon it. Just then, Ernest entered the room. He had heard my arrival and rushed over to welcome me. He expressed a mixture of sadness and joy at seeing me. "Welcome, my dearest Victor," he said. "Ah! I wish you had come three months ago, when we were all filled with joy and happiness. You've come to share in our sorrow, which nothing can ease. But I hope your presence will revive our father, who seems to be crumbling under his misfortune. And perhaps your words can convince poor Elizabeth to stop blaming herself incessantly. Oh, William! He was our beloved and our source of pride!"

Tears streamed down my brother's face, and a feeling of intense anguish overcame me. The sorrow of my destroyed home had been a mere figment of my imagination before, but now it hit me with a new and equally devastating force. I tried to calm Ernest down and asked for more details about our father, referring to him as my cousin.

"Most of all," Ernest said, "she needs comfort. She blames herself for our brother's death, and it's making her miserable. But now that the murderer has been found—"

"The murderer found! Impossible! How could anyone even attempt to pursue him? It's like trying to catch the wind or stop a rushing river with a straw. I saw him just yesterday, he was free!"

"I don't understand what you're saying," my brother replied, bewildered. "But for us, the discovery we've made only adds to our misery. No one believed it at first, and even now Elizabeth refuses to accept it, despite all the evidence. How could anyone believe that Justine Moritz, who was so kind and loved our family, could suddenly commit such a horrifying, appalling crime?"

"Justine Moritz! Poor girl, is she the one accused? But it's unjust; everyone knows it. Surely, Ernest, no one actually believes it?"

"At first, no one believed it, but then several details emerged that almost made it impossible to doubt her guilt. Her own actions were so perplexing that they only added more weight to the evidence, leaving little room for uncertainty. However, she will be tried today, and then you will hear everything."

He explained that on the morning when they discovered the murder of poor William, Justine had fallen ill and had to stay in bed for several days. During this time, one of the servants happened to examine the clothing she had worn on the night of the murder and found a picture of my mother in her pocket. This picture was believed to be the motive for the murderer. The servant immediately showed it to another servant, who, without informing the family, went to a magistrate. Based on their testimonies, Justine was arrested. When confronted with the accusation, the poor girl's extreme confusion largely confirmed their suspicions.

It was a strange story, but it didn't shake my belief. I responded fervently, "You are all mistaken; I know who the murderer is. Justine, poor, kind Justine, is innocent."

Right then, my father came into the room. I could see how sad he looked, but he tried to greet me with some cheerfulness. After we exchanged our sad hellos, he wanted to talk about something other than our disaster. But then Ernest exclaimed, "Oh my goodness, dad! Victor says he knows who killed poor William."

"We unfortunately know too," replied my father. "I would have preferred to remain ignorant forever rather than discover such wickedness and betrayal from someone I respected so much."

"No, dear father, you're mistaken. Justine is innocent."

"Well, if she is, then may God forbid that she should suffer as if she were guilty. She's going to be tried later today, and I hope, sincerely hope, that she will be found not guilty."

This statement made me feel more calm. I firmly believed in my heart that Justine, and every human being for that matter, was innocent of this murder. I had no fear that any evidence could be presented that would be strong enough to prove her guilt. My story was not one to be shared with the general public; its shocking horror would be seen as madness by most people. Did anyone besides myself, the creator, actually believe in the existence of the creature I foolishly unleashed into the world, if not for their own senses?

Elizabeth joined us not long after. She had changed since the last time I had seen her, growing into a beautiful young woman. Her character remained the same - open and lively - but there was now an added depth of sensitivity and intelligence in her expression. She greeted me with great affection. "Your arrival, my dear cousin," she said, "brings me hope. Perhaps you will find a way to prove the innocence of poor Justine. Who will be safe if she is wrongly convicted? I have complete faith in her innocence, just as I have faith in my own. Our misfortune is doubly painful; we have not only lost our beloved William, but this girl, whom I sincerely love, will also be taken away by an even worse fate. If she is condemned, I will never know joy again. But I am certain she will not be, and then I will be happy once more, even amidst the sorrow of William's death."

"She is innocent, Elizabeth," I assured her. "And we will prove it. Fear nothing, and find solace in the knowledge that she will be acquitted."

"How kind and generous you are! Everyone else believes her to be guilty, and that has caused me great misery, for I knew it couldn't be true. To see everyone else so prejudiced against her left me feeling hopeless and despondent." She began to cry.

"My dear niece," my father comforted her, "please don't cry. If Justine is truly innocent, you can rely on the fairness of our laws, and I will do everything in my power to ensure no hint of bias taints the proceedings."

EIGHT

113   WE SPENT a few sorrowful hours until eleven o'clock, when the trial was set to start. My father and the rest of the family had to go as witnesses, so I accompanied them to the courtroom. Throughout this miserable mockery of justice, I endured intense agony. The fate of two lives rested on the verdict: one, an innocent and joyful baby, the other, the victim of a horrific murder, stained with infamy that would make the crime unforgettable in its horror. Justine, too, was a girl of great worth, with qualities that promised a happy life. Now all of that was to be erased in a dishonorable grave, and I, the cause of it all! I would have confessed to being guilty of the crime attributed to Justine a thousand times over, but I was not present when it happened. Such a statement would have been seen as the ravings of a madman and would not have cleared her name, only further condemned her because of my involvement.

114   Justine looked calm and composed. She was dressed in black clothing, and her face, which was always charming, appeared even more beautiful due to the seriousness of her emotions. Despite being stared at and condemned by a crowd, she seemed confident in her innocence and did not tremble. The spectators were unable to see

past their belief in the terrible crime she was accused of. Any sympathy they might have felt for her beauty was erased from their minds. Although she appeared peaceful, it was clear that she was forcing herself to be that way. Previously, her confusion had been used as evidence against her guilt, so she made an effort to show bravery. As she walked into the courtroom, she scanned the room and quickly found where we were seated. A tear glistened in her eye when she saw us, but she swiftly regained her composure, and a look of sorrowful affection seemed to prove her complete innocence.

115   The trial began, and after the lawyer against Justine had presented the accusation, several witnesses were called. There were several strange facts that seemed to point against her, which might have made anyone doubt her innocence if they didn't have the evidence that I had. She had been out all night on the same night the murder happened, and a woman selling things at the market had seen her not far from where they later found the body of the murdered child. The woman asked Justine what she was doing there, but she seemed very strange and could only give a confused and unclear answer. Justine returned home around eight o'clock, and when someone asked her where she had been all night, she said she had been looking for the child and anxiously asked if they had heard any news about him. When they showed her the body, she had a violent hysterical reaction and stayed in bed for several days. They then presented a picture that the servant had found in Justine's pocket, and when Elizabeth, speaking in a hesitant voice, confirmed that it was the same picture that she had put around the child's neck an hour before he disappeared, the court burst into horrified murmurs.

Then it was Justine's turn to defend herself. As the trial went on, her expression changed. Surprise, horror, and misery were clearly visible on her face. Sometimes she fought back tears, but when it was time for her to speak up for herself, she gathered her strength and spoke with a voice that everyone in the court could hear, although it wavered at times.

"I swear to you that I am completely innocent," she said with confidence. "But I understand that my words alone may not be enough to prove it. I trust that my long-standing reputation as an upstanding individual will lead my judges to consider any uncertainties or suspicious circumstances in a positive light."

She then explained that, with Elizabeth's permission, she spent the evening of the night when the murder happened at her aunt's house in Chêne, a village about a mile away from Geneva. On her way back around nine o'clock, she encountered a man who asked if she had seen a missing child. This news frightened her, and she searched for several hours, but the gates of Geneva were already closed. Reluctant to disturb the residents who knew her, she had no choice but to spend the rest of the night in a barn near a cottage. She stayed awake, keeping watch until morning. She may have slept for a few minutes at dawn before being awoken by some noise. Not knowing the exact location where my brother's body was found, she couldn't have intentionally gone near it. It's not surprising that she seemed confused when questioned by the market-woman, as she had a sleepless night and wasn't sure what had happened to poor William. She had no explanation for the picture.

"I understand," continued the unhappy person, "how heavy and deadly this one detail weighs against me, but I have no way to explain it. When I've stated that I have no knowledge of it, I can only speculate about how it might have ended up in my pocket. But even there, I hit a roadblock. I don't think I have any enemies on earth, and certainly, no one would have been so wicked as to harm me for no reason. Did the murderer put it there? I can't think of any opportunity he would have had to do that. And even if he did, why would he have taken the jewel, only to get rid of it so quickly?

"I entrust my case to the fairness of my judges, but I don't see much hope. I request permission to have a few witnesses testify about my character. And if their testimony doesn't outweigh the presumption of my guilt, I will be condemned, even though I firmly believe in my innocence."

Several witnesses were called, people who had known her for many years, and they spoke positively about her. However, fear and hatred of the crime they believed she had committed made them hesitant and reluctant to come forward. Elizabeth saw that even this last chance, her good qualities and impeccable behavior, was about to fail her as the accused. Despite being deeply agitated, she mustered the courage to request permission to address the court.

119   "I am," she said, "the cousin of the young child who was murdered, or more accurately, his sister. I was raised by and have lived with his parents ever since before he was born. Some might view it as inappropriate for me to speak out in this situation, but when I witness a fellow human being on the verge of being condemned due to the cowardice of those who claim to be her friends, I feel compelled to speak up and share what I know about her. I am well acquainted with the accused. We lived together in the same house for a total of five years at one point, and nearly two years at another. Throughout that time, she struck me as the most kind-hearted and compassionate person. She took care of Madame Frankenstein, my aunt, with unwavering affection during her final illness. And later, she devoted herself to caring for her own mother during a long and difficult illness, earning the admiration of everyone who knew her. She then returned to live in my uncle's house, where she was cherished by the entire family. She had a deep bond with the child who tragically passed away and treated him with the utmost love and care, just like a devoted mother. As for the piece of jewelry that is the main evidence against her, if she had truly desired it, I would have gladly given it to her. That's how highly I regard and esteem her. Therefore, despite all the evidence presented against her, I firmly believe in her complete innocence."

120   Elizabeth's heartfelt plea drew murmurs of approval from the crowd. However, their approval was not in support of poor Justine, but rather in appreciation of Elizabeth's kind intervention. The public's anger now redirected towards Justine, accusing her of the worst kind of ingratitude. As Elizabeth spoke, Justine wept but

remained silent. Throughout the entire trial, I was deeply agitated and anguished. I firmly believed in Justine's innocence, knowing it to be true. Could the monster who, without a doubt, had murdered my brother also have betrayed the innocent to death and shame? I couldn't bear the horror of my situation any longer. When I saw that the public opinion and the judges' expressions had already condemned my unfortunate victim, I ran out of the courtroom in agony. The suffering endured by Justine did not compare to mine. She was sustained by her innocence, but the remorse inside me tore at my heart and refused to let go.

That night, I was consumed by pure misery. The next morning, I went to the courtroom, my lips and throat dry with fear. I couldn't bring myself to ask the fateful question, but the officer recognized me and understood why I had come. The votes had been cast - they were all black, and Justine was sentenced to death.

I can't begin to describe how I felt in that moment. I had felt horror before, and I tried to find words to express it, but nothing can capture the despair that consumed me. The person I spoke to then told me that Justine had already admitted her guilt. He said, "That evidence wasn't even necessary in such a clear-cut case, but I'm glad it's there. Our judges don't like to condemn someone based on circumstantial evidence, no matter how convincing it is."

This news was strange and completely unexpected. What did it mean? Was I seeing things wrong? Was I truly going mad, like the rest of the world would believe if I revealed what I suspected? I hurried back home, and Elizabeth anxiously asked for the outcome.

"My dear cousin," I replied, "it turned out as you might have expected. The judges would rather see ten innocent people suffer than let one guilty person go free. And she confessed."

This was a devastating blow to poor Elizabeth, who had whole-heartedly believed in Justine's innocence. "Oh no!" she exclaimed, "how can I ever trust in human goodness again? Justine, whom I loved and considered like a sister, how could she pretend to be innocent only to betray us? Her kind eyes seemed incapable of any cruelty or deceit, and yet she committed a murder."

Not long after, we learned that the unfortunate victim had expressed a wish to see my cousin. My father advised against it, but left the decision to her. "Yes," replied Elizabeth, "I will go, even though she is guilty. And, Victor, you must come with me. I cannot go alone." The thought of visiting Justine was painful to me, but I couldn't refuse.

We entered the dimly lit prison room and saw Justine sitting on some straw at the far end. Her hands were in chains, and she had her head bowed. She stood up when she saw us enter, and when we were alone with her, she fell to her knees in front of Elizabeth, crying uncontrollably. My cousin couldn't help but cry too.

"Oh, Justine!" Elizabeth exclaimed. "Why did you take away my last hope? I believed in your innocence, and though I was miserable at the time, I wasn't as hopeless as I am now."

"And do you also believe that I am so wicked? Are you joining forces with my enemies to crush me, to condemn me as a murderer?" Justine's voice was choked with sobs.

"Please, my poor girl, get up," said Elizabeth. "Why are you kneeling if you are innocent? I am not one of your enemies. I believed in your innocence despite all the evidence, until I learned that you admitted to your guilt. You say that report is false, and I assure you, dear Justine, that nothing can shake my faith in you, except your own confession."

"I did admit my guilt, but it was a lie. I confessed in order to receive forgiveness, but now that lie weighs heavier on my heart than all my other sins. May God forgive me! Since my conviction, my confessor has been pressuring me. He threatened and intimidated me, to the point where I almost believed I was the monster he claimed I was. He threatened me with excommunication and damnation in my final moments if I didn't relent. I had no one to support me; everyone saw me as a wretched person destined for shame and destruction. What could I do? In a terrible moment, I told a falsehood, and now I am truly miserable."

She paused, crying, and then continued, "I was horrified at the thought that you, my dear lady, would believe that Justine, whom your kind aunt held in such high esteem, and whom you loved, was capable of a crime that only the devil himself could commit. Dear William! Beloved child! I will soon see you again in heaven, where we will all be happy. That thought brings me comfort, even as I am about to suffer shame and death."

"Oh, Justine! Please forgive me for momentarily doubting you. Why did you confess? But do not grieve, dear girl. Do not be afraid. I will proclaim your innocence. I will prove it. I will soften the hardened hearts of your enemies through my tears and prayers. You will not die! You, my childhood friend, my companion, my sister, cannot perish on the scaffold! No! I could never survive such a terrible tragedy."

Justine sadly shook her head. "I'm not afraid to die anymore," she said. "That fear is gone. God gives me strength to endure the worst. I'm leaving behind a sad and bitter world. If you remember me, and see me as an innocent person wrongly accused, I am accepting of the fate that awaits me. Learn from me, dear lady, to patiently accept whatever God decides."

As they spoke, I retreated to a corner of the prison room where I could hide the terrible anguish that consumed me. Despair! Who dared speak of it? The poor victim, who was to cross the boundary between life and death the next day, didn't feel the same deep and bitter agony that I did. I clenched my teeth and groaned, the sound coming from deep within my soul. Justine noticed and approached me, saying, "Dear sir, you're very kind to visit me. Do you also believe that I'm guilty?"

I couldn't answer. "No, Justine," Elizabeth said. "He believes in your innocence even more than I did. Even when he heard that you had confessed, he didn't believe it."

"I truly appreciate that. In these final moments, I am deeply grateful to those who think kindly of me. The affection of others is so sweet, especially for a wretch like me. It lessens more than half of my misfortune. I feel as if I could die in peace now that you, dear lady, and your cousin acknowledge my innocence."

The poor sufferer tried to bring comfort to others, as well as herself. She did find the acceptance she sought. However, as the true murderer, I felt the unbearable guilt consuming me, leaving no room for hope or comfort. Elizabeth also wept and felt unhappy, but her misery stemmed from her innocence, like a passing cloud that briefly obscures the brightness of the moon but cannot diminish it. Agony and despair had penetrated deep into my heart, creating a living hell that could not be extinguished. We remained with Justine for several hours, and it was a struggle for Elizabeth to tear herself away. "I wish," she cried, "that I could die with you. I cannot live in this world of misery."

Justine put on a cheerful face, although she had to hold back her bitter tears. She embraced Elizabeth and said, with a voice filled with suppressed emotion, "Farewell, dear lady, beloved Elizabeth, my only friend. May Heaven, in its kindness, bless and protect you. May this be the last misfortune you ever endure! Live, be happy, and spread happiness to others."

And the next day, Justine died. Elizabeth's heartbreaking words failed to convince the judges of Justine's innocence. My impassioned pleas fell on deaf ears. Their cold responses and uncaring logic silenced my intended confession. I could declare myself insane, but I couldn't overturn the unjust verdict against my unfortunate victim. She met her end on the scaffold, labeled as a murderer.

As I suffered within the torment of my own conscience, I turned to see the profound and silent sorrow in Elizabeth's eyes. I was the cause of this too! My actions had resulted in the agony of my father and the destruction of our once joyful home. You weep, my dear ones, yet these tears won't be your last! The funeral dirge shall rise once again, and the sound of your mournful cries will echo repeatedly! Frankenstein, your son, your relative, your dear friend from early days, who would sacrifice every drop of his lifeblood for your sake, whose only happiness is reflected in the smiles on your faces, who wishes nothing but blessings upon you and devotes his life to serving you— he begs you to weep, to shed countless tears. He hopes that, if this merciless fate can be appeased, and if the torment can pause before it leads to the peace of the grave, it will bring some relief to your suffering!

This is what my soul told me. I felt regret, fear, and hopelessness while watching the people I cared about cry in sorrow at the graves of William and Justine, the first innocent victims of my forbidden experiments.

CHAPTER
NINE

128   NOTHING IS MORE agonizing to the human mind than when intense emotions give way to a state of complete stillness and certainty, leaving the soul without hope or fear. Justine passed away, finding peace in death, while I remained alive. Blood coursed through my veins, but my heart was burdened with feelings of despair and regret that couldn't be relieved. Sleep eluded me, and I roamed aimlessly like a troubled spirit, consumed by the dreadful deeds I had committed and convinced that there was even more wickedness to come. Despite this, my heart brimmed with kindness and a desire for virtuous acts. I had begun my life with noble intentions, eager for the opportunity to be helpful to others. But now, all hope was ruined. Instead of feeling a clear conscience and drawing inspiration for the future, I was consumed by remorse and guilt, pulling me into a torment that defies description.

This mental state took a toll on my health, which had never fully recovered from the initial shock it endured. I avoided the company of others, unable to bear hearing any expression of joy or contentment. Solitude became my only solace—a deep, dark, and deathly isolation.

129   My father noticed the change in my mood and actions, and tried to comfort me by explaining how he coped with difficult times through his own clear conscience and blameless life. He wanted to give me strength and courage to overcome the heaviness that consumed me. "Do you think, Victor," he said with tears in his eyes, "that I don't suffer too? I loved your brother more than anyone could love a child. But we have a responsibility to those still living, to not add to their sadness by showing excessive grief. It's also a responsibility to yourself because too much sorrow hinders progress, joy, and the ability to contribute to society."

His advice, though well-intentioned, didn't apply to me. If it weren't for my overwhelming remorse and fear, I would have tried to hide my grief and comfort my loved ones. Instead, I could only respond to my father with a look of despair and try to escape his sight.

130   During that time, we moved to our house in Belrive. This change was really nice for me. The strict curfew at ten o'clock and the rule that we couldn't stay on the lake past that time made living within the walls of Geneva really frustrating. But now I felt free. Many nights, after everyone else had gone to bed, I would take the boat out and spend hours on the water. Sometimes I would let the wind carry me with the sails, and other times, after rowing to the middle of the lake, I would let the boat drift while I drowned in my own miserable thoughts. There were moments when everything was peaceful around me, and I was the only restless thing in such a beautiful and heavenly scene. Except for maybe some bats or the frogs that made harsh croaking sounds when I got too close to the shore. In those moments, I felt tempted to dive into the quiet lake, letting the water close over me and my never-ending troubles. But I held back when I thought about Elizabeth, the brave and suffering person I loved deeply, whose life was tied to mine. I also thought about my father and my surviving brother. If I abandoned them by running away, they would be left vulnerable and unprotected against the monster I had unleashed upon them.

131   In those moments, I wept bitterly and longed for peace of mind so that I could bring them comfort and happiness. But it seemed impossible. Remorse consumed all hope. I was responsible for irreversible tragedies, and I lived in constant fear that the monster I had created would commit more wickedness. I had a nagging feeling that it was not over yet, and that he would perpetrate a heinous crime so atrocious that it would almost erase the memory of the past. As long as there was something or someone I cared about, fear could always find a way in. My abhorrence for this monster is indescribable. Just the thought of him made me grind my teeth, my eyes burn with anger, and I desperately wished to end the life I had so carelessly given him. When I pondered on his crimes and malice, my hatred and desire for revenge knew no bounds. If I could have, I would have traveled to the highest peak of the Andes and thrown him down to the base below. I longed to encounter him again, so I could unleash the full extent of my disgust upon him and avenge the deaths of William and Justine.

132   Our family was consumed by sadness. The recent events had severely impacted my father's health. Elizabeth was filled with sorrow and hopelessness. She couldn't find joy in her usual activities anymore. To her, any form of happiness felt disrespectful to the deceased. She believed that eternal grief and tears were the only fitting tribute to the innocence that had been so brutally taken away. She was no longer the cheerful person she used to be, who would explore the shores of the lake with me and dream about our future together. The first of many sorrows that are meant to detach us from earthly attachments had struck her, and its shadow had extinguished her warmest smiles.

133   "When I think about the sad death of Justine Moritz, my perspective on the world and its actions has completely changed. In the past, I saw stories of wrongdoing and unfairness in books or heard about them from others as tales of the past or made-up problems. They felt distant and easier to understand with reason rather than imagination. But now, suffering has come close to home, and

people seem like monstrous beings thirsty for each other's harm. However, I know I am being unfair. Everyone believed that poor girl was guilty, and if she had actually committed the crime for which she suffered, she would have been the most wicked of all human beings. To kill the son of her benefactor and friend, a child she had cared for since birth and loved as her own, all for a few jewels! I could never agree to the death of any person, but I would have thought someone like that unfit to be in society. But she was innocent. I am certain, and you sharing the same belief confirms it. Oh, Victor, when lies can appear so similar to the truth, how can we be certain of true happiness? I feel like I am walking on the edge of a dangerous cliff, with many trying to push me into the depths. William and Justine were murdered, and the killer remains free, maybe even respected. But even if I were sentenced to suffer on the gallows for the same crimes, I would not trade places with such a horrible person."

I listened to what she said with great pain. Although I was not the actual murderer, I felt deep guilt. Elizabeth could see my anguish in my face and kindly held my hand, saying, "My dear friend, you must calm down. These events have affected me too, but I am not as miserable as you are. There's a look of despair, and sometimes revenge, in your expression that makes me tremble. Victor, please get rid of these dark emotions. Remember the friends who care about you and put all their hopes in you. Have we lost the ability to make you happy? Ah! As long as we love each other and stay true here in our peaceful and beautiful homeland, we can have a peaceful life. What can disturb our happiness?"

And couldn't her words, coming from someone whom I cherished more than anything else, be enough to chase away the evil thoughts in my heart? As she spoke, I moved closer to her, as if in fear that at that very moment, the destroyer was about to take her away from me.

However, neither the love of friendship, nor the beauty of the earth, nor the beauty of the sky could free my soul from sadness.

Even the loving words were ineffective. I was surrounded by a cloud that no positive influence could break through. I felt like a wounded deer, dragging its tired legs to a hidden place, there to look at the arrow that had pierced it, and to die.

135   Sometimes I could handle the overwhelming despair that consumed me. Sometimes physical activity would help me. It was during one of these times that I suddenly left my home and decided to head towards the nearby Alpine valleys. I hoped that the grandeur and timeless beauty of these places would help me forget about my own temporary, yet very human, sorrows. I specifically directed my wanderings towards the valley of Chamounix, a place I had visited many times during my childhood. Although six years had passed since then and I was now a broken individual, nothing had changed in those wild and enduring landscapes.

136   I began my journey on horseback, but then I decided to hire a sturdy mule because they are less likely to get hurt on these rough roads. The weather was nice. It was around mid-August, about two months after Justine's death, which marked the start of my suffering. As I ventured deeper into the Arve ravine, the weight on my spirit started to lighten. The towering mountains and cliffs surrounding me, the roaring sound of the river rushing through the rocks, and the thundering waterfalls all spoke of a power so great that I could only think of it as almighty. I no longer feared or felt inferior to anything or anyone but the creator of the elements displayed in their most terrifying form. As I climbed higher, the valley became even more magnificent and awe-inspiring. Abandoned castles hanging on the cliffs of pine-covered mountains, the fast-flowing Arve River, and scattered cottages peeking out from the trees created a scene of unique beauty. But what made it truly breathtaking were the mighty Alps, their snow-covered peaks and shining domes towering above everything else, as if they belonged to a different world, a home for a different race of beings.

137   I crossed the Pélissier bridge and began climbing the mountain that loomed above the ravine formed by the river. Soon after, I

entered the valley of Chamounix. This valley was even more impressive and awe-inspiring, though not as picturesque and charming, as the Servox valley I had just passed through. The towering snow-capped mountains formed its boundaries, devoid of any ruined castles or fertile fields. Enormous glaciers approached the road, as I heard the thunderous rumble of the avalanches and witnessed the smoke left in their wake. Mont Blanc, the majestic and supreme peak, rose above the surrounding peaks, dominating the valley.

During this journey, I would sometimes feel a long-lost sense of pleasure. A sudden turn in the road or the sight of a familiar object would evoke memories of days long gone, bringing back the carefree joy of my youth. The gentle whispers of the wind and the nurturing embrace of nature would console me, bidding me to stop shedding tears. But then, that comforting influence would fade away—I would find myself once again bound to sorrow, sinking into the depths of despair as I indulged in painful introspection. In those moments, I urged my horse forward, desperate to forget the world, my fears, and most of all, myself—or, in a more desperate state, I dismounted and collapsed onto the grass, overwhelmed by horror and hopelessness.

Finally, I reached the village of Chamounix. I was completely exhausted from both the physical and mental fatigue that I had endured. I stood at the window for a brief moment and admired the faint lightning illuminating the sky above Mont Blanc. The rushing sound of the Arve River below provided a soothing background noise. It calmed my heightened emotions and acted as a lullaby. When I finally lay my head on my pillow, sleep slowly engulfed me. I could feel it approaching and I appreciated the relief it brought, allowing me to forget my troubles.

CHAPTER
TEN

139   I SPENT the next day exploring the valley. I stood beside the origins of the Arveiron, which starts from a glacier that slowly moves down from the top of the hills to block the valley. There were steep sides of immense mountains in front of me. The glacier's frozen wall loomed above me. A few broken pine trees were scattered around. The only sounds that disturbed the solemn silence of this majestic room of nature were the rushing waves or the crash of large pieces of ice falling, the thunderous roar of avalanches, or the echoing cracks as the ice shattered and tore apart due to the unchanging laws of nature. These awe-inspiring and magnificent scenes gave me the greatest comfort that I was capable of feeling. They lifted me above any small or insignificant emotions. Although they didn't take away my grief, they subdued and calmed it. To some extent, they also distracted my thoughts from the things I had been brooding over for the past month. I went to bed that night with images of grand forms that I had observed during the day almost guiding my sleep. They gathered around me—the pure white mountain peak, the sparkling summit, the pine forests, and rugged open gorge, the majestic eagle soaring

through the clouds. They all surrounded me and whispered for me to find peace.

140 The next morning, I woke up wondering where all the soul-inspiring beauty had gone. Sleep had taken it away, leaving behind a dark melancholy that clouded my thoughts. The rain was pouring down heavily, and thick mists covered the mountain peaks, making it impossible to see their majestic faces. But I was determined to find them in their cloudy hideaways. The rain and storm meant nothing to me. My mule was brought to the door, and I made up my mind to climb to the top of Montanvert. I remembered how the sight of the immense and ever-moving glacier had filled me with awe when I first saw it. It had given me a sense of sublime ecstasy, lifting my soul from the gloomy world to a place of light and joy. The presence of the majestic and awe-inspiring in nature had always had a way of solemnizing my mind, making me forget about the worries of daily life. I decided to go alone, as I knew the path well, and having someone else with me would take away from the solitary grandeur of the scenery.

141 The ascent is very difficult and it requires taking many short paths in order to get around. It is a scene terrifically desolate. Additionally, trees lie broken and strewed on the ground, with some entirely destroyed, others bent, leaning upon the jutting rocks of the mountain. The paths, as you ascend higher, are surrounded by snow and steep cliffs. The pines are not tall or luxuriant, but they are sombre, and add an air of severity to the scene. I looked on the valley beneath: vast mists were rising from the rivers which ran through it. While rain poured from the dark sky, it added to the melancholy impression I had about these surroundings. What a thought! We are moved by every wind that blows, and a chance word or scene that that word may convey to us.

142 We take a break; a dream can ruin our sleep.

We wake up; one lingering thought ruins the day.

We experience, understand, or think; laugh or cry,

Embrace deep sadness, or let go of our worries;

It's all the same: whether it's happiness or sadness,
It will eventually fade away.
A person's past may never be the same as their future;
Nothing lasts forever except change!

143 It was almost noon when I reached the top of the hill. I sat on a rock, looking out over the icy sea. A mist covered everything, including the surrounding mountains. But soon a breeze blew the cloud away, and I made my way down onto the glacier. The surface was rough, with waves and deep cracks. The icy field stretched for about a mile, and it took me almost two hours to cross it. On the other side, there was a sheer rock mountain. From where I stood, Montanvert was directly across, about a mile away. And towering above it was Mont Blanc, looking terrifyingly majestic. I found a little spot in the rock to hide, and I couldn't stop staring at this incredible and amazing sight. The icy river twisted among the mountains, their peaks shining brightly in the sunlight above the clouds. My sad heart suddenly felt a hint of joy. I said to myself, "If wandering spirits truly exist and don't rest in their graves, let me have this small happiness or take me with you, away from the joys of life."

144 As I said this, I suddenly saw a man coming towards me with incredible speed. He easily jumped over the cracks in the ice that I had been cautiously avoiding. And as he got closer, it seemed like he was taller than an average person. It startled me: my vision blurred and I felt a wave of faintness come over me. But the cold mountain wind quickly revived me. As the figure got closer (a terrifying and repugnant sight!), I realized it was the creature I had brought to life. I trembled with a mix of anger and horror, deciding to confront him in a fight to the death. He drew near. His face showed both intense suffering and contempt, with an unearthly ugliness that made it almost unbearable to look at. However, rage and hatred had taken away my ability to speak, and I only regained it to unleash a torrent of furious loathing and scorn upon him.

"You devil," I cried out, "do you dare to come near me? Don't you fear the fierce wrath of my hand that will punish your wretched head? Leave, you vile creature! Or better yet, stay so I can crush you into dust! And oh, if only I could bring back to life those innocent souls you have so diabolically murdered!"

145 "I knew you would react this way," said the creature. "Everyone despises the miserable, so how much more must they hate me, who am the most wretched creature alive! Yet, you, my creator, detest and reject me, your own creation, bound to each other in a way that can only be broken by the death of one of us. You plan to kill me. How dare you play with life like this? Do your duty towards me, and I will do mine towards you and the rest of humanity. If you agree to my terms, I will leave you and your loved ones alone, but if you refuse, I will satisfy death's hunger by spilling the blood of your remaining friends."

"You monstrous, abhorrent fiend! The pains of hell are too lenient a punishment for your crimes. Pitiful devil! You speak ill of me for creating you, so come, let me end the spark that I carelessly bestowed."

I was consumed by anger, driven by every emotion that could fuel one being's hatred for another.

He easily dodged me, and said --

146 "Calm down! Please listen to me before you release your anger on me. Haven't I already suffered enough? Life, even if it's filled with only anguish, is precious to me and I will fight to protect it. Remember that you made me more powerful than yourself - taller and more flexible. But I won't be tempted to go against you. I am your creation and I will be obedient and gentle towards my natural leader if you fulfill your responsibilities towards me. Frankenstein, don't treat everyone else fairly and trample on me alone, when I deserve your fairness, mercy, and affection the most. Remember that I am your creation; I should be your Adam, but I am more like a fallen angel whom you cast away without cause. Everywhere I see happiness that I am forever excluded from. I used to be kind and good, but misery turned me into a monster. Make me happy, and I will be virtuous once again."

"Go away! I won't listen to you. There can be no understanding between us; we are enemies. Leave, or we can test our strength in a fight where only one of us will fall."

147   "How can I make you understand? Will you not listen to my pleading, as I implore you for kindness and compassion? Believe me, Frankenstein: I was once good-hearted; my soul was filled with love and care for others. But now I am all alone, horribly alone. You, my creator, despise me; what hope can I find from your fellow humans, who owe me nothing? They reject and detest me. I seek solace in the desolate mountains and icy caves. They are my refuge, the only places where I don't face scorn. I welcome these harsh skies, for they treat me better than your fellow humans do. If the world knew of my existence, they would do as you do and arm themselves to destroy me. Shouldn't I then hate those who hate me? I refuse to have any kind of relationship with my enemies. I am miserable, and they will suffer with me. But you have the power to make it right and save them from a catastrophe, one that you alone can make so severe that not only you and your family, but thousands of others, will be consumed by its fury. Show compassion and do not reject me. Hear my story: once you have listened, decide if you should abandon me or feel pity towards me, depending on what you believe I deserve. But please, listen to me. Even the guilty have the chance to defend themselves before they are condemned by human laws, cruel as they may be. Listen to me, Frankenstein. You accuse me of murder, and yet you, with a clear conscience, would dismantle your own creation. Oh, how remarkable is the justice of mankind! But I am not asking for mercy: just listen to me, and then, if you can and if you want to, destroy what you have made with your own hands."

148   "Why do you bring up memories," I replied, "that I cannot bear to think about? Memories that remind me that I am the miserable one who caused all of this pain? Cursed be the day, you accursed creature, when you first came into existence! Cursed (even as I curse myself) be the hands that created you! You have made me incredibly unhappy. You have taken away my ability to even consider if I have

treated you justly or not. Go away! Spare me from having to look at your detested form."

"This is how I spare you, my creator," he said, and covered my eyes with his hated hands, which I forcefully pushed away from me. "By doing this, I take away a sight that you despise. But you can still listen to me and show me compassion. I demand this from you based on the virtues I once possessed. Hear my story; it is long and strange, and the conditions here are not suitable for your delicate senses. Come to the hut on the mountain. The sun is still high in the sky; before it sets behind those snowy cliffs, casting light on another world, you will have heard my story and can make a decision. It is up to you whether I walk away forever from human company and live a harmless life, or become a terror to your fellow humans and the cause of your own quick demise."

As he said this, he led the way across the ice, and I followed. My heart was filled with emotions, and I didn't respond to him. Instead, I considered the different points he made and decided to at least hear his story. My curiosity pushed me to listen, and my compassion confirmed my decision. Until now, I had thought he was responsible for my brother's death, and I wanted to know the truth. For the first time, I also understood the responsibilities a creator has towards their creation and realized that it was important to ensure his happiness before accusing him of wrongdoing. These reasons pushed me to grant his request. We crossed the ice and climbed the opposite rock. The air was chilly, and the rain started to fall again. We entered the hut, with the fiend appearing victorious and me feeling burdened and downcast. However, I agreed to listen and settled myself by the fire that my detestable companion had lit. And so, he began his tale.

ELEVEN

150   "It is quite difficult for me to recall the exact time when I came into existence: all the events from that period seem jumbled and unclear. I was overwhelmed by a strange mix of sensations, experiencing sight, touch, hearing, and smell all at once. It took me a while to learn how to distinguish between these different senses. Gradually, I remember a brighter light starting to intensify, making me close my eyes. Darkness then enveloped me, causing some unease, but as soon as I opened my eyes, the light flooded back in. I walked, and I believe I descended, but I soon realized a significant change in my sensations. Previously, I was surrounded by dark and solid objects that I couldn't touch or see through, but now I discovered that I could freely move without any hindrances that I couldn't either overcome or avoid. The light became too much, and the heat exhausted me as I walked, so I looked for shade. This happened to be the forest near Ingolstadt, where I rested beside a stream. I ate some berries that I found hanging from the trees or scattered on the ground. I quenched my thirst at the stream, and then lay down, succumbing to sleep."

151   When I woke up, it was dark and I felt cold. I was also scared and lonely. Before leaving the room, I had wrapped myself in some

clothes to keep warm, but they weren't enough to protect me from the nighttime cold. I was a poor, helpless, and miserable person. I couldn't see or understand anything, but I felt pain all around me, so I sat down and cried.

Soon, a gentle light started to appear in the sky, bringing me a feeling of joy. I stood up and saw a bright figure emerge from the trees. I looked at it with wonder. It moved slowly, but it illuminated my path. I decided to go out and look for berries again. I was still cold, but then I found a large cloak under one of the trees. I covered myself with it and sat down on the ground. My mind was in a confusion, with no clear thoughts. I felt light, hungry, thirsty, and surrounded by darkness. I heard many different sounds and smelled various scents all around me. The only thing I could really see was the bright moon, and I stared at it happily.

Several days and nights went by and I started to recognize my different feelings. I slowly saw the clear stream that gave me water, and the trees that provided shade with their leaves. I felt happy when I first realized that a pleasant sound I often heard came from the little winged creatures that sometimes blocked my view. I also began to observe more closely the shapes around me and understand the limits of the bright sky that covered me. Sometimes I tried to copy the joyful songs of the birds, but I couldn't succeed. Sometimes I wanted to express my own feelings, but the strange and unclear sounds that came out of me scared me back into silence.

The moon had disappeared from the night sky and then appeared again, smaller than before, while I was still in the forest. By then, my feelings became clearer and my mind learned new things every day. My eyes got used to the light and were able to see objects in their correct shapes. I could tell the difference between insects and plants, and eventually, I could even distinguish one type of plant from another. I discovered that sparrows made harsh sounds, while blackbirds and thrushes sang sweet and captivating songs.

One day, when I was very cold, I found a fire that had been left behind by some beggars who had passed by. I was filled with joy when I felt the warmth from the fire. In my excitement, I put my hand into the burning embers, but quickly pulled it back because it hurt. I thought it was strange that the same thing could cause such different effects. I examined the fire and was happy to discover that it was made of wood. I gathered some branches, but they were wet and wouldn't catch fire. I felt disappointed and sat there, watching how the fire worked. As the wet branches got closer to the heat, they dried out and eventually caught fire. I thought about this and used my hands to test different branches to understand why. Then I got busy collecting a lot of wood so that I could dry it out and have plenty of firewood. When it got dark and time for sleep, I was afraid that my fire would go out. I carefully covered it with dry wood and leaves, and I put wet branches on top of it. Then I spread out my jacket and lay on the ground, falling asleep.

154   In the morning, when I woke up, my first task was to check on the fire. I uncovered it, and a gentle breeze quickly helped it turn into a flame. I noticed this and came up with an idea to use branches as a fan to revive the dying embers. When nightfall came once again, I was pleased to find that the fire not only provided warmth but also gave off light. I also discovered that this newfound element was helpful in preparing my food. Some leftovers from the travelers had been roasted by the fire and tasted much better than the berries I had been picking from the trees. So, I decided to try cooking my food in the same way, placing it on the live embers. I realized that the berries didn't turn out well with this method, but the nuts and roots tasted much better.

155   However, finding enough food became a challenge. Many times, I would spend the entire day searching, but could only find a few acorns to ease my hunger. When I eventually found them, I decided it was time to leave the place I had been living in and search for somewhere else. During this journey, I deeply regretted losing the fire that I had stumbled upon by accident and had no idea how to recreate it. I wrapped myself in my cloak and headed westward across the forest. I wandered for three days and eventually discov-

ered an open area. It had snowed heavily the night before, and the fields were now covered in a white blanket. The overall appearance was quite gloomy, and I could feel the cold and dampness of the snow chilling my feet as I walked.

It was early in the morning, around seven o'clock, and I was desperate for some food and shelter. After some time, I spotted a small hut on a hill, which seemed to have been built for a shepherd's convenience. This was a completely new sight for me, and I felt a great sense of curiosity as I examined the structure. With the door open, I decided to go inside. Inside the hut, there was an old man sitting near a fire, preparing his breakfast. As he heard a noise, he turned and noticed me, causing him to shriek loudly. Without any hesitation, he quickly left the hut and started running across the fields, surprising me with his speed despite his weak appearance. I was intrigued by his unusual reaction and his fleeing. However, I was captivated by the hut itself. It provided a sanctuary where the snow and rain couldn't get in, and the ground was dry. At that moment, the hut seemed like a heavenly retreat, just as Pandæmonium would have appeared to the demons of hell after their sufferings in the lake of fire. I eagerly ate the remaining bits of the shepherd's breakfast, which consisted of bread, cheese, milk, and wine, although I didn't particularly enjoy the wine. Exhausted, I laid down on some straw and soon drifted off to sleep.

It was around noon when I woke up, and the warmth of the sun on the snowy ground tempted me to continue my journey. I packed the leftover food from the shepherd's breakfast into a bag I discovered and set off across the fields for several hours. At sunset, I reached a village, and it seemed like a marvelous sight to me. The simple houses and grander buildings captured my admiration. The sight of vegetables in the gardens and milk and cheese on cottage windows enticed my hunger. I decided to enter one of the nicer cottages, but as soon as I stepped inside, the children screamed, and one of the women fainted. The entire village was in an uproar. Some people ran away, and some attacked me. Injured from being hit with stones and other objects, I managed to escape to the open country-side. In fear, I sought refuge in a run-down and bare hovel, a stark contrast to the beautiful houses I had seen in the village. This hovel was made of wood and was so short that it was hard for me to sit up straight. The floor was just the earth, but it was dry. Even though the wind came through countless cracks, it provided a pleasant shelter from the snow and rain.

158   So there I went, finding comfort in the fact that I had discovered some sort of refuge from the harsh weather and the cruelty of people.

In the morning, I emerged from my makeshift dwelling, eager to get a glimpse of the nearby cottage and determine if I could stay there. It was positioned against the back of the cottage, near a pig-sty. I had entered through an open part, but now I covered any gaps that might expose me with stones and wood, leaving enough room to move them aside when needed. The only light that illuminated my space came from the sty, but it was enough for me.

With my dwelling arranged and comfortably lined with clean straw, I retreated inside. I spotted a man in the distance, prompting me to recall the mistreatment I had endured the previous night and causing me to be careful of putting myself in his hands. Before settling in, though, I made sure to secure my sustenance for the day - a loaf of coarse bread that I discreetly took, and a cup to drink from, which was much more convenient than using my hands, thanks to the nearby flowing water. The floor of my refuge was slightly elevated, ensuring it stayed dry, and its proximity to the cottage's chimney provided some warmth.

159   With the provisions I had acquired, I made up my mind to stay in this humble dwelling until something came along that might change my decision. Compared to the harsh forest where I used to live, with its dripping branches and damp ground, this place truly felt like paradise. I enjoyed my breakfast and was about to remove a plank to get myself some water, when I heard footsteps. Through a small crack, I caught a glimpse of a young girl with a pail on her head,

walking past my hovel. Unlike the cottagers and farm workers I would encounter later, she had a gentle demeanor. However, she was dressed plainly, wearing a simple blue skirt and a plain linen jacket. Her fair hair was neatly braided but lacked any adornments. She seemed patient yet sorrowful. I lost sight of her, but about fifteen minutes later, she returned with the pail, now partially filled with milk. As she struggled with the burden, a young man approached her, his face displaying even deeper sadness. With a mournful expression, he took the pail off her head and carried it to the cottage himself. She followed him, and they disappeared from view. Soon, I spotted the young man once again, holding some tools as he crossed the field behind the cottage. The girl, too, was busy, alternating between tasks inside the house and out in the yard.

Upon examining my new dwelling, I discovered that one of the cottage's windows had been replaced with wood. However, there was a small chink in one of the wooden panels, barely noticeable, that allowed for a glimpse inside. Through this opening, I could see a small, clean room with white walls, though it lacked much furniture.

In a corner of the room, near a small fire, an elderly man sat with his head in his hands, appearing deeply sad. The young girl, meanwhile, was busy arranging things in the cottage. But at one point, she retrieved something from a drawer and sat down next to the old man. They both started to play instruments, producing melodies that were more beautiful than the songs of a thrush or a nightingale. It was a breathtaking sight for me, a person who had never witnessed anything so lovely before.

The old man had silver hair and a kind face that commanded my respect, while the girl's gentle demeanor filled me with affection. He played a melancholy tune that brought tears to the girl's eyes. The girl cried and the old many comforted her. He lifted her up, smiling with such kindness and affection that I experienced an over-whelming mix of pain and pleasure unlike anything I had ever felt before. It was a sensation that was new for me. Unable to bear these intense emotions, I stepped away from the window.

161   Not long after, the young man returned with a bundle of wood on his back. The girl greeted him at the door and helped him unload. They carried some of the wood inside and added it to the fire. Then they went to a corner of the cottage to talk privately. The young man showed her a large loaf of bread and a piece of cheese, which made her happy. She went to the garden and picked some roots and plants, which she put in water and cooked over the fire. While she continued her work, the young man went to the garden and diligently dug up more roots. They spent about an hour working separately until the young woman joined him and they entered the cottage together.

162   The old man had been lost in thought, but when his companions arrived, he put on a happier expression. They sat down to eat quickly. The young woman started tidying up the cottage, while the old man took a short walk in the sun, leaning on the young man's arm. The contrast between the two of them was striking. The old man had silver hair and a face filled with kindness and love, while the younger man had a slim and graceful figure with perfectly proportioned features. However, his eyes and posture showed deep sadness and despair. The old man went back into the cottage, and the young man grabbed different tools from earlier and headed across the fields.

163   As night fell, I was amazed to discover that the cottagers had a way to keep light glowing using candles. I was thrilled to realize that when the sun went down, I could still enjoy watching my human neighbors. In the evening, the young girl and her companion were doing things that I couldn't quite understand, and the old man picked up his instrument again to produce the beautiful sounds that had captivated me in the morning. Once he finished, the young man began to make sounds that didn't resemble the harmony of the old man's instrument or the songs of birds. Later, I learned that he was reading aloud. However, at that time I didn't know anything about words or letters.

After a short while, the family put out their lights and went to bed, as I guessed.

CHAPTER
TWELVE

164   I LAY on my bed of straw, but I couldn't sleep. I couldn't stop thinking about everything that happened that day. What stood out the most to me was how kind and polite these people were. I wished I could join them, but I was too afraid. The memory of the villagers' cruel treatment from the night before was still fresh in my mind. So, for now, I decided to stay hidden in my small, rundown shelter. I would observe them closely, trying to understand their actions and motivations.

The next morning, the family woke up before the sun rose. The young woman cleaned and organized the cottage, while also preparing the food. After the first meal, the young man left the cottage for the day.

The day passed in a similar way to the previous one. The young man busied himself with outdoor tasks, while the girl worked on various demanding chores inside the cottage. The old man, who I realized was blind, spent his free time playing his instrument or lost in thought. The deep affection and respect the young cottagers showed for their elderly companion was extraordinary. They performed every act of love and duty towards him with great care, and he rewarded them with kind smiles.

They were not completely happy. The young man and his companion would often separate and seem to cry. I couldn't understand why they were so unhappy, but it deeply affected me. If such beautiful beings were miserable, then it made sense for me, an imperfect and alone being, to also be miserable. But why were these gentle beings unhappy? They lived in a lovely house (at least, in my eyes) and had every luxury. They had a fire to keep them warm when it was cold, and delicious food when they were hungry. They dressed in excellent clothes, and most importantly, they enjoyed each other's company and showed affection and kindness. So why were they crying? Did their tears show pain? At first, I couldn't figure out these questions, but with constant observation and time, I began to understand the mysteries.

It took a long time before I discovered one of the reasons for this kind family's unhappiness: it was poverty. They suffered greatly from this terrible circumstance. Their only food came from the vegetables in their garden and the small amount of milk from their cow. The cow didn't produce much during the winter, when it was difficult for the family to find enough food for it to survive. They often experienced intense hunger, especially the two younger members of the family. There were multiple occasions when they would provide food for the old man, but wouldn't keep any for themselves.

This act of kindness touched me deeply. In the past, during the night, I used to sneak some of their food for myself. But when I saw that it caused pain for the family, I stopped and satisfied my hunger with berries, nuts, and roots that I found in a nearby forest.

I also discovered another way to help them with their work. I noticed that the young man would spend most of his day gathering firewood for the family. So, at night, I would take his tools and quickly learn how to use them. I would then bring home enough firewood to last them for several days.

I remember the first time I did this, the young woman was

greatly surprised when she opened the door in the morning and saw a large pile of wood outside. She exclaimed in a loud voice, and the young man joined her, also expressing surprise. I was pleased to see that he didn't have to go to the forest that day, but instead spent it repairing the cottage and working in the garden.

167   I gradually made an even more important discovery. I realized that these people had a way of sharing their experiences and emotions with each other through spoken words. I noticed that the words they spoke sometimes brought joy or sadness, smiles or frowns to those who heard them. It was a remarkable skill, and I desperately wanted to understand it. But every attempt I made to do so ended in frustration. They spoke quickly, and the words they used didn't seem to be connected to anything I could see, making it impossible for me to decipher their meaning. However, after spending many months in my small dwelling, I managed to learn the names they used for some common objects. I learned and used words like fire, milk, bread, and wood. I also discovered the names of the people living in the cottage. The young man and his companion had multiple names, while the older man was only called father. The girl went by sister or Agatha, and the young man was known as Felix, brother, or son. I cannot describe the joy I experienced when I finally understood the concepts behind each of these words and could pronounce them. I recognized some other words as well, though I didn't yet comprehend their meaning or how to use them, like good, dearest, and unhappy.

168   I spent the winter like this. The kind and beautiful nature of the people living in the cottage made me adore them. Their sadness made me feel down, and their happiness made me share in their joy. I didn't see many other humans besides them, but when someone else happened to come into the cottage, their rude behavior and awkward movements only made me appreciate my friends' superior qualities even more. I could tell that the old man often tried to encourage his children, whom he sometimes referred to as such, to overcome their sadness. He would speak in a cheerful tone. Agatha

listened respectfully, sometimes with tears in her eyes that she tried to discreetly wipe away. But I noticed that her face and voice were usually more cheerful after listening to her father's encouraging words. Felix, on the other hand, was always the most sorrowful one in the group. Even to me, he seemed to have endured more pain than his friends. But despite his sorrowful face, his voice was more upbeat than his sister's, especially when speaking to the old man.

I saw many examples of the kind-hearted nature of these lovely cottagers. Despite their poverty, Felix would joyfully bring the first little white flower he found underneath the snow to his sister. Every morning, even before she woke up, he would clear the snow from her path to the milk-house, fetch water from the well, and bring in wood from the out-house. To his constant surprise, he would always find the wood replenished by an unseen hand. During the day, he often worked for a nearby farmer and wouldn't return until dinner, but he never brought back any wood. When there wasn't much to do in the winter months, he would read to the old man and Agatha in the garden.

At first, I couldn't understand the reading at all. However, I realized that he made the same sounds when he read as he did when he spoke. I guessed that he recognized these sounds as signs for speech on the paper, and I desperately wanted to understand them too. However, how could I when I didn't even understand the sounds they represented? I did make some progress in learning this skill, but not enough to have a proper conversation. Even though I tried my best, I knew that I couldn't reveal myself to the cottagers until I could speak their language. Knowing their language might make them look past the way I looked.

I admired the perfect appearances of the cottagers—how graceful, beautiful, and fair-skinned they were. But then, I was terrified when I saw myself in a clear pool. At first, I recoiled, unable to believe that the reflection in the mirror was truly me. When I finally accepted that I was indeed the monster that I am, I felt a deep sense of hopelessness and embarrassment. Little did I know, however, just how devastating the effects of this dreadful deformity would be.

171   As the sun grew warmer and the days got longer, the snow melted away, revealing the bare trees and the dark soil. From that point on, Felix had more tasks to do, and the worrying signs of a coming food shortage disappeared. Their meals, I later discovered, were plain but nourishing, and they always managed to get enough to eat. New types of plants started to grow in the garden, which they took care of, and these signs of comfort increased day by day as the season progressed.

At noon, if it wasn't raining, which I learned is what they called it when the sky released its water, the old man would go for a walk, leaning on his son for support.

172   In my little shack, my daily routine was always the same. In the morning, I watched what the cottagers were doing, and when they went off to do different things, I took a nap. The rest of the day, I spent observing my friends. Once they had gone to bed, if there was a moon or the night was clear and full of stars, I would venture into the woods to find food and gather firewood for the cottage. Whenever I came back, if it was necessary, I would clear their path from the snow and do the same tasks I had seen Felix do. Later on, I realized that these invisible deeds greatly surprised them, and a couple of times I overheard them say the words kind spirit and amazing. However, I didn't understand the meaning of these words back then.

173   As I lived in my small home, my daily routine was steady. In the morning, I watched the cottagers go about their tasks. When they were all occupied with their own work, I would sleep. The rest of the day, I would observe my friends. When they went to sleep, I would venture into the woods to gather food and fuel for the cottage. Whenever necessary, I would clear the snow from their path and perform the tasks I had seen Felix do. I later discovered that these invisible labors greatly amazed them. I overheard them utter words like "good spirit" and "wonderful" on these occasions. However, I did not understand what they meant at the time.

Now, my curiosity grew even stronger, and I yearned to understand the motives and emotions of these lovely individuals. I longed to know why Felix seemed so unhappy and Agatha so sorrowful. Foolishly, I thought that I might have the power to bring happiness back into their lives. When I slept or was away, I would imagine the kind, blind father, the gentle Agatha, and the excellent Felix. I saw them as superior beings who held the key to my future. In my mind, I painted countless scenarios of introducing myself to them and how they would receive me. I imagined that they might be repulsed by me at first, but through my kind demeanor and friendly words, I would win their favor and ultimately their love.

These thoughts filled me with joy and motivated me to work even harder to learn their language. My vocal abilities were far from perfect, but I managed to pronounce the words I understood fairly well. It was like the comparison between an mule and a dog. Even though my voice wasn't nice, I hope they'd treat me well.

174

The arrival of spring brought about a delightful transformation to the earth. People, who had previously seemed to hide in caves, now spread out and engaged in various activities related to farming. The birds sang in more cheerful melodies, and the leaves started to grow on the trees. The earth, once bleak, damp, and unhealthy, became a happy and welcoming place. It was as if the land, in such a short time, had become suitable even for gods. Witnessing this wondrous change in nature lifted my spirits. I forgot about the past, finding peace in the present, and felt hopeful and excited about what the future had in store for me.

CHAPTER

THIRTEEN

175   I NOW HURRY to the more emotional part of my story. I will share events that deeply affected me, shaping me into the person I am today.

Spring progressed quickly. The weather turned pleasant, and the skies were clear. It amazed me how the once empty and gloomy surroundings now blossomed with the most beautiful flowers and greenery. I was delighted and refreshed by countless delightful scents and captivating sights.

It was on one of these days, when my neighbors took a break from their work— the old man played his guitar, and the children listened to him— that I noticed a profound sadness in Felix's expression. He sighed often, and at one point, his father paused his music, and seemed to ask of his son's sorrow. Felix responded cheerfully, and the old man was about to resume his music when someone knocked on the door.

176   A lady on a horse, with a local guide, approached the cottage. She was wearing a dark outfit and had a thick black veil covering her. Agatha asked a question, to which the stranger responded by softly saying Felix's name. Her voice was pleasant, but different from both

of my friends. When Felix heard his name, he quickly approached the lady. As soon as she saw him, she lifted her veil, revealing a face of breathtaking beauty and emotion. She had shiny black hair, intricately braided, and her eyes were dark, yet kind and lively. Her facial features were well-proportioned, and her complexion astonishingly fair, with a lovely pink blush on each cheek.

Felix's face lit up with joy when he saw her, all traces of sadness disappeared, and he looked as though he was in a state of pure happiness. His eyes shimmered and his cheeks flushed with delight. At that moment, I thought he was as lovely as the lady. She seemed to be moved by different emotions; she wiped a few tears from her eyes and reached out her hand to Felix, who kissed it passionately. He called her, as far as I could hear, his dear Arabian. She didn't seem to understand him, but she smiled. He helped her off the horse and, after sending her guide away, led her into the house. There was some conversation between him and his father, and the young stranger knelt at the old man's feet. She tried to kiss his hand, but he raised her up and hugged her lovingly.

I quickly realized that even though the stranger spoke in understandable words and seemed to have her own language, neither she nor the cottagers understood each other. They exchanged many gestures that I couldn't understand, but I could see that her presence brought joy to the cottage, just like how the sun disperses morning mist. Felix was especially happy and warmly welcomed the stranger. Agatha, always gentle, kissed the stranger's hands and pointed at her brother, signaling that he had been sad until she arrived. Hours passed in this way, with joyful expressions on their faces. Soon, I noticed that the stranger was trying to learn their language by repeating certain sounds they made. It immediately occurred to me that I should do the same to learn as well. During the first lesson, the stranger learned about twenty words, most of which I already understood, but I also learned from the others.

As evening arrived, Agatha and the Arabian retired early. When they said their goodbyes, Felix kissed the stranger's hand and bid her a good night. He stayed up longer, conversing with his father. I desperately longed to understand them, but despite my best efforts, it was impossible.

The following morning, Felix left for work, and after Agatha finished her usual tasks, the Arabian sat at the old man's feet. With her guitar in hand, she played melodies that were incredibly beautiful.

When she finished, she offered the guitar to Agatha, who initially declined. She played a simple tune and sang with sweet accents, although not as wondrous as the stranger's earlier performance. The old man appeared captivated and spoke some words. Agatha tried to explain them to Safie, conveying that her music brought him immense delight.

180 The days now passed peacefully, with one significant change: joy replaced sadness in the faces of my friends. Safie was always cheerful and content. She and I made rapid progress in learning the language, so much so that within two months, I began to understand most of the words spoken by my protectors.

Meanwhile, the grass grew and the sun became much warmer. My nighttime strolls became a great source of pleasure, although they were shortened by the sun rising early and setting late. I avoided going outside during daylight, fearing the mistreatment I had experienced in the first village I entered.

During the day, I diligently focused on learning the language, allowing me to make progress more quickly than the Arabian, who understood very little and struggled to speak fluently. I, on the other hand, comprehended and could imitate nearly every word I heard.

As my speech improved, I also delved into the world of written language, as the stranger taught me. This opened up a vast realm of awe and excitement for me.

181 "The book that Felix used to teach Safie was called 'Ruins of Empires' by Volney. I wouldn't have understood the purpose of this book if Felix hadn't provided detailed explanations while reading it. He chose this book because it was written in a dramatic style that

imitated eastern authors. From reading this book, I gained a basic understanding of history and learned about the different empires that exist in the world today. It also gave me a glimpse into the customs, governments, and religions of various nations. It gave me a tour of lands, people, and their history. I even heard about the discovery of the Americas and felt sadness with Safie for the unfortunate fate of its original inhabitants."

These amazing stories made me feel a mix of emotions. It was hard to understand how humans could be both powerful and virtuous, yet also wicked and base. For a long time, I couldn't understand why people would harm or kill each other, or even why there were laws and governments. But when I learned about the details of vice and violence, I stopped wondering and instead felt disgusted and repulsed.

Listening to the conversations of the people living in the cottages brought me even more amazement. I learned about the strange way human society is organized. I heard about how wealth and poverty are divided, about social classes, family lineage, and the importance of having noble ancestors.

The words made me think about myself. I learned that the things most valued by people were having a good family background and being wealthy. If a person had either one of these things, they could be respected. But if they didn't have either, they were seen as a wanderer and a servant, forced to use their abilities for the benefit of the privileged few! And what was I? I had no idea about my origin or who created me. I knew that I had no money, no friends, and no possessions of any kind. On top of that, I had a horribly deformed and repulsive appearance. I wasn't even the same species as humans. I was stronger and could survive on simpler food. I could tolerate extreme temperatures better than them, and I was also taller. When I looked around, I saw and heard about no one like me. So, was I a monster? A disgrace to the earth that everyone ran away from and disowned?

I can't even begin to describe the pain these thoughts caused me. These realizations were too much.

184   How strange knowledge can be! Once it grabs hold of your mind, it sticks to it like a plant on a rock. Sometimes, I wished I could just get rid of all thoughts and emotions. But I learned that the only way to escape the pain was death, a state that I was afraid of and didn't fully understand. I admired good values and kind-heartedness, and I loved the gentle manners and likable qualities of the people in the cottage. However, I was shut off from interacting with them, except for the times when I secretly observed them without being seen or known. These brief moments only intensified my longing to become a part of their society. The kind words of Agatha and the cheerful smiles of the charming person from Arabia were not meant for me. The gentle advice from the old man and the lively conversations with the beloved Felix were not meant for me either. I was a miserable, unhappy person!

Other lessons impacted me even more deeply. I learned about the differences between males and females, and how children are born and grow up. I discovered how fathers dote on their babies' smiles and the playful antics of older children. I saw how a mother's whole life revolves around her precious children. I witnessed the way young minds expand and gain knowledge. I learned about brothers, sisters, and all the different connections that bring human beings together in mutual bonds.

185   But where were my loved ones? No father had watched over my early years, no mother had showered me with affectionate smiles and embraces, or if they had, all memories of them were now hazy, a void in which I could distinguish nothing. Since as long as I could remember, I had always been the same in height and build. I had never encountered another person who resembled me, or who claimed any connection to me. Who was I? The question echoed in my mind, with only my anguished groans as a response.

I will soon explain the purpose behind these emotions, but for now, let me return to the humble residents of the cottages, whose tale evoked within me a mix of anger, joy, and astonishment, yet ultimately deepened my love and admiration for my guardians (for that is how I perceived and innocently, albeit somewhat painfully, referred to them).

CHAPTER

FOURTEEN

186   IT TOOK me a while to find out what happened to my friends. Their story left a deep impression on me, as it revealed many fascinating and extraordinary details that someone as inexperienced as myself found captivating.

The man's name was De Lacey, and he came from a respected family in France. He had enjoyed a life of wealth and was held in high regard by both his superiors and peers. His son had served in the military, while Agatha was well-regarded among the distinguished ladies. Just a few months before I met them, they had been living in the glamorous and bustling city of Paris, surrounded by friends and enjoying all the pleasures that came with their virtues, intelligence, refined tastes, and modest wealth.

Safie's father was the reason behind their downfall. He was a merchant from Turkey who had been living in Paris for many years. For some unknown reason, he had become a target of the government. On the very day that Safie arrived from Constantinople to join him, he was arrested and thrown into prison. He was put on trial and sentenced to death. The injustice of his punishment was evident, and the whole city of Paris was outraged. Many believed that it was his religion and wealth, rather than the alleged crime, that led to his condemnation.

Felix happened to be at the trial by accident. He was filled with horror and anger when he heard the court's decision. In that moment, he made a solemn vow to rescue the prisoner and began searching for a way to do so. After several unsuccessful attempts to enter the prison, he discovered a heavily barred window in an unguarded area of the building. The window provided light to the cell of the unfortunate Muslim man, who was chained and waiting in despair for his cruel punishment to be carried out. Felix started visiting the window at night and revealed his plan to help the prisoner. The Turk was amazed and grateful, trying to motivate Felix by promising him wealth and rewards. However, Felix rejected these offers with disdain. Yet, when he saw Safie, the beautiful daughter who was allowed to visit her father, and witnessed her expressing her deep gratitude through gestures, Felix couldn't help but admit to himself that the captive possessed a treasure that would be worth all the effort and risk.

The Turk quickly realized the impact Safie had on Felix's heart and tried to win him over completely by offering her hand in marriage once they were both safe. Felix, however, was too honorable to accept this offer directly, but he couldn't help but dream of the possibility becoming a reality, which would bring him ultimate happiness.

In the following days, as the merchant planned his escape, Felix received several letters from the beautiful girl. She found a way to communicate with the help of an elderly servant who understood French. In these letters, she expressed her deepest gratitude for Felix's assistance to her father and also expressed her sadness about her own situation.

I managed to acquire writing materials while I stayed in the shanty, so I have copies of these letters. Felix and Agatha often had them in their possession. Before I leave, I will give you the letters as proof of my story. However, as the day is turning late, I only have enough time to give you a summary of their contents.

189 Safie told the story of her mother, who was a Christian Arab taken captive and enslaved by the Turks. Despite her circumstances, her beauty captured the heart of Safie's father, who married her. Safie spoke highly and passionately about her mother, who had been born free and resented the enslavement imposed upon her. Her mother taught Safie about her religion and encouraged her to strive for intellectual growth and independence. Safie's mother passed away, but her teachings left a lasting impact on Safie's mind. Safie despised the idea of returning to Asia and being confined. Therefore, the prospect of marrying a Christian and living in a country where women were granted social standing excited her.

The day of the Turk's execution was set, but on the night before, he escaped from prison and, by morning, had traveled many miles away from Paris. Ahead of time, Felix obtained passports for himself, his father, and sister. He had already shared his plan with his father, who cooperated by leaving their home under the pretense of going on a trip. They hid themselves, along with his daughter, in a secluded area of Paris.

190 Felix led the refugees across France to Lyons, and through Mont Cenis to Leghorn. It was there that the merchant decided to wait for a suitable opportunity to enter the Turkish territories.

Safie made up her mind to stay with her father until his departure. The Turk reassured her that she would be united with her rescuer before he left. Felix remained with them in anticipation of that moment. In the meantime, he enjoyed the company of the Arabian woman, who showed him the purest and most heartfelt affection. They communicated through an interpreter and sometimes with the exchange of glances. Safie also sang him the beautiful songs of her homeland.

The Turk permitted this close bond to develop and encouraged the young lovers' hopes. However, deep inside, he had different intentions. He despised the idea of his daughter marrying a Christian, but he feared Felix's anger if he showed any reluctance. He knew that his fate still rested in the hands of his rescuer, who could expose him to the Italian authorities. The Turk devised countless plans to prolong the deception until it was no longer necessary, secretly intending to bring his daughter with him when he left. His schemes were made easier by the news that arrived from Paris.

The French government were very angry that their prisoner had escaped and they made every effort to find and punish the person who helped him. Felix's plan was quickly discovered, and De Lacey and Agatha were put in prison. When Felix heard the news, it snapped him out of his happy daydream. His elderly father and kind sister were stuck in a dark, smelly jail cell, while he got to enjoy freedom and spend time with the woman he loved. This thought tortured him. He quickly made an agreement with the Turks. If they found a good chance to escape before Felix could return to Italy, Safie would stay at a convent in Leghorn. Then, without wasting any more time with his beloved Arabian, he rushed to Paris and turned himself in to the law, hoping that by doing so, he could free De Lacey and Agatha.

However, his plan did not work. They were kept in confinement for five months before their trial took place, and the outcome was that they lost all their money and were forced to leave their home-land forever.

They found a sad place to live in a small cottage in Germany, where I later found them. Felix quickly learned that the deceitful Turk, who had caused countless suffering to him and his family, had become a traitor to decency and honor. He had left Italy with his daughter and had the audacity to send Felix a small amount of money, claiming it was to help him find a way to support himself in the future.

These were the events that deeply affected Felix, making him the most miserable in his family when I first met him. He could have handled being poor, and in fact, he took pride in his virtue despite the hardships. But the Turk's ingratitude and the loss of his beloved

Safie were even more painful and impossible to fix. The arrival of the Arabian girl brought a renewed sense of hope to his weary spirit.

When word reached Leghorn that Felix had lost his wealth and social status, Safie's father ordered her to forget about her lover and prepare to go back to her home country. Safie, being a generous person, was outraged by this command and tried to reason with her father. But he angrily left, repeating his tyrannical demand.

A few days later, the Turk came into his daughter's room in a rush and told her that he had reason to believe that his presence in Leghorn had been discovered. He feared being handed over to the French government, so he had rented a ship to take him to Constantinople. He would leave his daughter in the care of a trusted servant and she could join him later when most of his belongings, which hadn't arrived in Leghorn yet, were ready.

"When she was by herself, Safie thought about what she should do in this difficult situation. She didn't want to stay in Turkey because it went against her religion and her feelings. She found some papers from her father and learned that her lover had been forced to leave and knew where he was staying. She thought about it for a while, but finally made up her mind. She took some of her jewelry and money and left Italy with her attendant, who was from Leghorn and could speak the language of Turkey. They went to Germany.

They made it to a town about twenty leagues from De Lacey's cottage when her attendant got very sick. Safie took care of her with a lot of love, but sadly, the attendant died. Now, Safie was all alone and didn't know the language of the country or anything about how things worked there. But she ended up in good hands. The Italian had told her the name of the place they were going, and after the attendant died, the woman who owned the house where they stayed made sure Safie got safely to her lover's cottage."

FIFTEEN

"THIS IS the story of the people who lived in the cottages that I loved. It made a big impression on me. It showed me the good qualities of people that I admired and made me dislike their bad qualities.

So far, I thought of crime as something far away. Kindness and generosity were always in front of me, inspiring me to join in the busy world where so many great qualities were shown. But as I talk about how my mind developed, I can't forget what happened in the beginning of August that same year.

One night, when I went to the nearby forest to get food for myself and bring back wood for my protectors, I found a bag on the ground. Inside were clothes and some books. I was excited and took the bag back to my home. Luckily, the books were written in the language I learned at the cottage. They were 'Paradise Lost,' a book about famous people called 'Plutarch's Lives,' and 'The Sorrows of Werter.' I was extremely happy to have these treasures. While my friends were busy with their normal tasks, I spent my time studying and thinking about these stories."

The effect of these books on me was indescribable. They filled my mind with countless new images and emotions that sometimes brought me great joy, but more often plunged me into deep sadness. In the book 'Sorrows of Werter,' aside from the captivating and touching story, there were discussions and insights into topics that were previously unclear to me. This book became an endless source of wonder and contemplation for me. The gentle and family-oriented way of life it depicted, along with its noble ideals and aspirations that went beyond personal interests, resonated deeply with my experiences with my caretakers and with the longings that I carried within myself. I thought Werter himself was a more extraordinary being than anyone I had ever seen or imagined. His character possessed no pretenses, but it had a profound impact on me. The discussions about death and suicide were bewildering, and while I couldn't fully grasp the complexities of the arguments, I found myself leaning toward the viewpoints of the hero, whose own demise I mourned, albeit not entirely comprehending it.

196   As I read, though, I related much of what I read to my own feelings and situation. I saw similarities between myself and the characters I encountered in the books, yet I also felt strangely different from them. I sympathized with them and partly understood their experiences, but my mind was still developing. I didn't rely on anyone and didn't have any close relationships. "The path of my departure was free," and there was no one to mourn or miss me if I were to disappear. I was physically repulsive and abnormally tall. What did this mean? Who was I? What was I? Where did I come from? What was my purpose? These questions kept coming up, but I couldn't find any answers.

197   The book I had in my possession was called "Plutarch's Lives." It was about the founders of the ancient republics and it had a different impact on me compared to "The Sorrows of Werter." While Werter's story made me feel sad and hopeless, Plutarch's book inspired me with lofty thoughts. It took me beyond my own limited perspective and allowed me to admire and respect the heroes of the past.

However, there were many things in the book that I didn't fully understand. I knew very little about kingdoms, countries, rivers, and seas, but I had no knowledge of towns or large gatherings of people. The only exposure I had to human nature was through the lens of my protectors' cottage. Reading this book opened my eyes to new and grander experiences of human action. I learned about people involved in politics and making important decisions for their communities, as well as those who caused harm and destruction. This ignited a strong desire for virtue within me and a deep aversion to vice, as far as I could understand those concepts in relation to pleasure and pain.

Because of these emotions, I naturally found myself admiring peaceful lawgivers like Numa, Solon, and Lycurgus more than warriors like Romulus and Theseus. The way my protectors lived their lives also influenced these perspectives. If my first encounter with humanity had been through a young soldier seeking glory and bloodshed, I might have developed different feelings.

However, "Paradise Lost" evoked different and much stronger emotions within me. I read it, just like the other books I had come across, as if it were a true account. It stirred up a sense of wonder and awe. I found myself relating to various situations in the story, recognizing their resemblance to my own experiences. Similar to Adam, it seemed as though I had no connection to any other being in existence. But in every other aspect, our circumstances were vastly different. Unlike me, Adam was a flawless and content creature, created by God himself. He enjoyed protection and guidance from his Creator, and could engage in conversations and gain knowledge from beings of a superior nature. On the contrary, I was miserable, vulnerable, and alone. I had no creator to protect me. Beyond this, I was jealous and often confused.

Another thing further strengthened and confirmed these feelings. Shortly after I arrived in the small, rundown shelter, I discovered some writings in the pocket of the dress that I had taken from your laboratory. At first, I didn't pay much attention to them; but now that I could understand the words they were written in, I started to study them with great care. They were your journal entries from the four months leading up to when I was created. In these papers, you meticulously described every single step you took in your work, and you also included details about daily life. I'm sure you remember these papers. Here they are. They contain everything related to my wretched origin; every horrific detail of the events that led to it is laid out before me. The papers even include a detailed description of my repulsive and disgusting appearance, described in a way that vividly conveyed your own horrors and made my own even more unforgettable. I became sickened as I read. "What a dreadful day it was when I came to life!" I cried out in agony. "Cursed creator! Why did you bring to life a monster so repulsive that even you turned away from me in disgust? God, in His mercy, made humans beautiful and alluring, reflecting His own image. But my form is a hideous reflection of yours, even more horrifying in its resemblance. Satan had his companions, other devils, to admire and support him. But I am alone and despised."

200   These were my thoughts during my times of feeling down and lonely. However, as I observed the kind and caring nature of the people living in the cottage. I convinced myself that if they were to learn about my admiration for their virtues, they would feel sorry for me and overlook my physical deformity. Could they reject someone, even if they were monstrous, who asked for their compassion and friendship? I made a decision not to give up and to make myself ready for a meeting with them that would determine my destiny. I delayed because I was afraid of failing, considering how crucial it was for me to succeed. Additionally, I noticed that my understanding was getting better each day, so I didn't want to start this endeavor until a few more months had passed and I had gained more wisdom.

201   Meanwhile, some changes occurred in the cottage. Safie's presence brought happiness among the people living there, and there seemed to be more abundance. Felix and Agatha spent more time enjoying themselves and talking, and they had servants to help with their work. They didn't seem wealthy, but they were content and happy, having peaceful and serene feelings, while my own emotions

became more chaotic with each passing day. The more I learned, the more I realized how much of an outcast I was. Though I clung to hope, it disappeared when I saw my reflection in water or my shadow in the moonlight, just like a fragile image or an ever-changing shadow.

I tried to suppress these fears and prepare myself for the trial I had decided to face in a few months. Sometimes, I let my thoughts wander without restraint into the realms of paradise, imagining kind and beautiful beings who understood and comforted me, dispelling my gloom with their angelic smiles. But it was all a fantasy; there was no Eve to comfort me or share my thoughts—I was alone. I remembered Adam's plea to his Creator, but where was mine? He had abandoned me, and in my bitterness, I cursed him.

Autumn went by like this. I watched in surprise and sadness as the leaves decayed and fell, and nature once again took on the barren and desolate look it had when I first saw the woods and the beautiful moon. Yet, I didn't mind the cold weather as much; my body was better suited to endure cold rather than heat. But my greatest joys came from seeing the flowers, the birds, and all the vibrant colors of summer. When those things left, I turned my attention more towards the people in the cottages. Their happiness didn't diminish with the absence of summer. They loved and cared for each other, and their joys, dependent on one another, weren't interrupted by the unfortunate events that occurred around them. The more I saw of them, the stronger my longing grew to seek their protection and kindness. My heart yearned to be known and loved by these kind-hearted beings. I wished to see their affectionate looks directed towards me. I didn't dare think that they would turn away from me with disdain and horror. The poor who sought their help were never turned away. It's true that I asked for more than just food and rest—I longed for kindness and understanding—but I didn't believe myself to be completely unworthy of it.

As autumn turned to winter, I noticed the changing seasons since I came into existence. My focus now was on finding a way to enter the cottage where my protectors lived. I thought of different plans, but settled on the idea of approaching the blind old man when he was alone. I understood that my appearance was what scared people the most. However, I believed that if I could gain the trust and support of the old De Lacey, I might be accepted by his children.

One day, when the sun was shining on the red leaves scattered across the ground, Safie, Agatha, and Felix went on a long walk in the countryside. The old man chose to stay behind in the cottage. Once his children were gone, he picked up his guitar and played several sad yet beautiful melodies, more soulful than I had ever heard from him before. At first, his face showed delight, but as he continued playing, his expression became thoughtful and melancholic. Eventually, he set aside the instrument and sat there lost in deep contemplation.

204 My heart raced; this was the moment that would determine whether my hopes would come true or my fears would be realized. The servants had gone to a nearby fair, leaving the cottage quiet and empty. It was the perfect opportunity, but as I tried to execute my plan, my legs gave way and I fell to the ground. I gathered my strength and got up, removing the planks I had used to conceal my hiding place. The fresh air revived me, and with renewed determination, I approached the cottage door.

I knocked. "Who is it?" said the old man. "Come in."

I entered and said, "I apologize for this intrusion. I am a traveler in need of some rest. It would greatly help me if you could allow me to warm up by the fire for a few minutes."

"Please come in," De Lacey said. "I'll do my best to help you, but I'm afraid my children are not home, and as a blind man, it might be difficult for me to find food for you."

"No need to worry, kind sir. I have food; all I require is warmth and rest."

I sat down, and silence filled the room. Time was of the essence, but I couldn't decide how to start the conversation. Then, the old man spoke up.

"Judging by your language, I assume you are from my country. Are you French?"

"'No, but I was educated by a French family, and understand that language only. I am now going to claim the protection of some friends, whom I sincerely love, and of whose favour I have some hopes.'

"'Are they Germans?'

"'No, they are French. But let us change the subject. I am an unfortunate and deserted creature. I look around, and I have no relation or friend upon earth. These people to whom I go have never seen me, and know little of me. I am full of fears, for if I fail there, I am an outcast in the world for ever.'

"'Do not despair. To be friendless is indeed to be unfortunate, but the hearts of men, when unprejudiced, are full of brotherly love and goodness. Rely, therefore, on your hopes; and if these friends are good and amiable, do not despair.'

"'They are kind—they are the most excellent creatures in the world, but, unfortunately, they are prejudiced against me. When they look at me, they behold only a detestable monster.'

"'That is indeed unfortunate; but if you are really blameless, cannot you undeceive them?'

"I am about to take on that task, and that's why I feel so many overwhelming fears. I deeply care for these friends. I have been kind to them every day for many months without their knowledge. But they believe that I want to harm them, and it's that prejudgment that I want to overcome."

"Where do these friends live?"

"Nearby."

The old man stopped and then continued, "If you will tell me all the details of your story, I might be able to help change their minds. I am blind, so I can't rely on your appearance, but something in your words convinces me that you are telling the truth. I am poor and an outcast, but it would give me true pleasure to be of help to another human being."

"You're an amazing person! I appreciate your kindness and accept your generous offer. You uplift me with this act of kindness, and I hope that, with your assistance, I won't be excluded from society and the support of other people."

"God forbid! Even if you were truly guilty, it would only push you to desperation, not towards virtue. I, too, have been unlucky. My family and I have been unfairly condemned. So judge for yourself if I don't understand your misfortunes."

"How can I express my gratitude, my kindest and most generous benefactor? You are the first person to show me kindness and it warms my heart. I will be forever thankful to you, and I truly believe that with your help, I will be able to win over my friends whom I am about to meet."

"May I know the names and where these friends live?"

I hesitated. This was the critical moment, which would determine whether I would find happiness or lose it forever. I struggled to compose myself to respond, but my efforts only drained me further. I could not hold back my emotions any longer and collapsed into the chair, sobbing uncontrollably. In that very moment, I heard the footsteps of my younger protectors approaching. There was no time to waste. Desperately, I grasped the old man's hand and pleaded, "Now is the time! Please save and protect me! You and your family are the friends I have been searching for. Please, do not abandon me in this difficult moment!"

"Oh my goodness!" the old man exclaimed. "Who are you?"

At that exact moment, the door of the cottage swung open, and Felix, Safie, and Agatha walked in. It's impossible to describe the sheer terror and shock they experienced upon seeing me. Agatha couldn't handle it and fainted, while Safie, too overwhelmed to assist her friend, hurried out of the cottage. Felix lunged forward and separated me from his father, to whom I desperately clung. Consumed by rage, he violently threw me to the ground and struck me with a stick. I had the urge to retaliate, but overcome by pain and anguish, I fled

from the cottage, taking advantage of the chaos to slip away unnoticed to my hovel.

CHAPTER
SIXTEEN

 "WHY DID I continue to live? Why didn't I just end my own existence when I had the chance? I don't know. Despair hadn't fully taken over me yet; anger and a desire for revenge consumed me instead. I took pleasure in imagining destroying the cottage and its inhabitants, reveling in their screams and suffering.

"When night fell, I left my hiding place and wandered through the woods. Now, free from the fear of being discovered, I unleashed my anguish in howls that would send shivers down anyone's spine. I was like a wild animal breaking free from its restraints, destroying anything that stood in my way and sprinting through the forest with the swiftness of a deer. Oh, what a wretched night I endured! The cold stars above mocked me, and the bare trees swayed their branches as if taunting me. Every now and then, I would hear the sweet song of a bird piercing through the silence. Everyone, except me, seemed at peace or enjoying their lives. But I, like a demon, carried a personal hell within me. When I found no sympathy from anyone, I wished to uproot the trees, cause chaos and havoc all around me, and then sit back and relish in the destruction."

 However, this pleasurable experience did not last long. I soon grew exhausted from the physical exertion and collapsed on the damp grass, overcome by despair. Among the countless humans who existed, there was no one who would pity or assist me. Should I feel any kindness towards my enemies? No. From that moment, I declared an eternal war against humanity. I heard the voices of people and knew that I couldn't return to my hiding place until nightfall. Therefore, I found a hidden spot in the thick underbrush and decided to spend the following hours reflecting on my situation.

The pleasant sunshine and fresh daylight brought some peace to my troubled mind. When I considered what had happened at the cottage, I couldn't help but think that I had been too rash in my judgments. I had definitely acted imprudently. It was clear that my conversation had intrigued the father and gained his sympathy, and I was foolish to reveal myself to the terrified children. I should have gradually gained the trust of the elderly De Lacey and then introduced myself to the rest of the family when they were prepared. But I believed that my mistakes were not irreversible. After careful consideration, I made up my mind to return to the cottage, find the old man, and convince him to side with me through persuasive arguments.

These thoughts calmed me, and in the afternoon I fell into a deep sleep. However, my restless state prevented me from having peaceful dreams. The terrifying events of the previous day continued to replay in my mind; the women were fleeing and Felix, filled with rage, was tearing me away from his father. I woke up feeling exhausted. Realizing it was already nightfall, I left my hiding spot and went in search of food.

Once my hunger was satisfied, I made my way towards the familiar path that led to the cottage. Everything was quiet there. I sneaked into my small shelter and waited in silence, anticipating the usual time when the family would wake up. That time came and went, the sun rose higher in the sky, but the cottagers did not appear. I shook with fear, fearing some terrible misfortune. The inside of the cottage was dark and I heard no movement. I cannot begin to describe the agony of this uncertainty.

Suddenly, two men from the countryside passed by. They paused near the cottage and engaged in a conversation filled with animated gestures. However, I couldn't understand what they were saying, as they were speaking the local language that was different from that of my protectors. Shortly after, Felix approached with another man. I was taken aback, as I knew he hadn't left the cottage that morning. I anxiously waited to hear their conversation, hoping to understand the meaning behind these unusual appearances.

212   "Do you think," asked Felix's friend, "that you will have to pay three months' rent and lose the produce from your garden? I want to be fair, so I suggest you take some time to think about your decision."

"It's pointless," replied Felix. "We can never live in your cottage again. My father's life is in great danger because of what happened. My wife and sister will never recover from the horror. Please don't try to argue with me anymore. Take back your property, and let me escape from here."

Felix shook with fear as he spoke. He and his friend went inside the cottage, stayed for a few minutes, and then left. I never saw any of the De Lacey family again.

213   "I spent the rest of the day in my small and miserable shelter, feeling completely hopeless and filled with despair. The people who had been taking care of me had left, severing the only connection I had to the outside world. For the first time, I was consumed by feelings of revenge and hatred, and I didn't even try to suppress them. I allowed myself to be swept away by these dark emotions, fixating on causing harm and death. But whenever thoughts of my friends, like De Lacey's soothing voice, Agatha's gentle eyes, and the beautiful Arabian, came to mind, my anger would dissipate and I would find some solace in tears. Yet, every time I remembered how they had rejected and abandoned me, that anger would return, fiercer than ever. Unable to harm any human being, I redirected my fury towards

objects around me. As night fell, I strategically placed various flammable materials around the cottage. After destroying all signs of the garden that had been cared for, I impatiently waited for the moon to set so I could begin my destructive plan."

As the night grew darker, a strong wind emerged from the woods, swiftly pushing away the lingering clouds in the sky. The gust raced through like a powerful avalanche, causing a frenzy in my emotions. I lit a branch from a dry tree and spun around the cottage in a fit of rage. Eventually, a portion of the moon disappeared, and I swung my makeshift torch. As it sank, I let out a loud cry and ignited the collected straw, heath, and bushes. The wind intensified the flames, and they quickly consumed the cottage, licking it with their deadly tongues.

Once I realized that there was no hope for any part of the dwelling to be saved, I left the site and sought refuge in the woods.

And now, with the whole world spread out in front of me, where should I go? I made up my mind to escape from the place where all my misfortunes had happened. But no matter where I went, every country would feel the same - hateful and despising towards me. Then I remembered you. Your papers told me that you were my father, my creator. Who else could I turn to but the one who gave me life? Felix had taught Safie geography, so I knew where the different countries were. You mentioned Geneva as your hometown, and that's where I decided to go.

But how would I find my way? I knew I had to travel in a south-westerly direction, but I had no idea of the names of the towns I would pass through. And I couldn't ask anyone for help. But I didn't lose hope. I knew I could only rely on you, even though all I felt for you was hatred. Heartless creator! You gave me senses and emotions, and then left me to face the disdain and horror of humanity. But you were the only one I could ask for help and justice. I had tried in vain with others who looked like humans, but all my hope was in you.

My journey was lengthy, and the hardships I endured were severe. It was late in the fall when I left the area where I had been staying for a long time. I only traveled during the night, afraid of coming across another person. The natural surroundings decayed around me, and the sun lost its warmth; rain and snow poured down on me, powerful rivers froze, the ground was hard, cold, and bare, and I couldn't find any shelter. Oh, how many times did I curse the reason for my existence! The gentleness in my personality disappeared, and bitterness filled every part of me. The closer I got to your home, the stronger the desire for revenge burned within me. Despite the falling snow and frozen waters, I didn't stop. Occasionally, a few incidents helped guide me, and I had a map of the area, but I often strayed far from my intended path. The agony of my emotions gave me no relief. Every event fueled my anger and misery, but a particular incident that occurred when I reached the border of Switzerland, where the sun had regained its warmth and the earth began to turn green again, intensified my bitterness.

217 "I usually rested during the day and only traveled at night to avoid being seen by people. However, one morning I found myself passing through a dense forest and decided to continue my journey after the sun had risen. It was a beautiful spring day, filled with warm sunshine and a gentle breeze. I was amazed to feel a sense of gentleness and happiness that I thought had long been gone. It was a new and unfamiliar emotion for me, and I couldn't help but surrender to it. For a moment, I forgot about my loneliness and appearance, and allowed myself to be truly happy. Tears of joy streamed down my face, and I even looked up at the sun with gratitude for bringing such happiness into my life."

218 I continued to walk through the paths of the woods until I reached its edge, which was bordered by a deep and fast river. Many of the trees had branches that bent towards the river, with fresh buds of spring. Unsure of which way to go, I stopped and heard voices nearby. I quickly hid under the shade of a cypress tree. As I hid, I saw a young girl running towards me, laughing as if she were playing a game. She kept running along the steep sides of the river when suddenly she slipped and fell into the fast-moving water.

Without hesitation, I rushed out of my hiding spot, fought against the strong current, and saved her, pulling her to safety on the shore. She was unconscious, and I did everything I could to revive her. Just as I was trying to help her regain consciousness, a farmer approached. He was probably the person she was running away from in their game. When he saw me, he ran towards me, forcefully taking the girl from my arms, and quickly disappearing deeper into the woods. I followed closely behind, not knowing why, but as I got closer, he pointed his gun at me and fired. I fell to the ground, and the man ran away even faster into the woods.

This was the terrible consequence of my kindness! I had rescued a person from danger, and as a result, I now suffered from a painful wound that broke my flesh and bone. I swore to forever despise and seek revenge against all humanity. But the agony of my injury overpowered me; my heart slowed, and I lost consciousness.

For several weeks, I endured a wretched existence in the woods, attempting to heal the wound I had sustained. I was uncertain if the bullet had lodged in my shoulder or passed through it, but regardless, I had no means to remove it. The weight of the injustice and ingratitude I had endured only added to my suffering.

After a few weeks, my wound finally mended, and I resumed my journey. The hardships I faced could no longer be eased by the warmth of the sun or the gentle breezes of spring. Any joy felt like a mockery that taunted my lonely state and reminded me that I was not meant to experience happiness.

But now, my trials were approaching their end and in just two months from that point, I arrived in the outskirts of Geneva.

It was getting dark when I arrived at Geneva, and I found a secluded spot in the fields to think about how I should approach you. I was exhausted and hungry, too miserable to appreciate the pleasant evening breeze or the stunning view of the mountains.

In my troubled state, I was partially relieved by a short nap. However, my rest was interrupted by the arrival of a young child, full of playful energy, who ran into the hiding spot where I was. As I looked at the child, an idea struck me: this innocent little being had not yet learned to fear or judge based on appearances. Perhaps, if I could take him and raise him as my companion and friend, I would feel less isolated in this crowded world.

Driven by this notion, I grabbed the boy as he passed by and pulled him towards me. But the moment he saw my face, he covered his eyes and let out a piercing scream. I forcefully removed his hands from his face and said, "Child, there's no need to be afraid. I don't mean you any harm. Listen to me."

He fought back desperately. "Let go of me!" he shouted. "You're a monster! A hideous creature! You want to eat me and tear me apart! You're an ogre! Let me go, or I'll tell my father!"

"Boy, you won't see your father again," I replied firmly. "You must come with me."

"You ugly monster! Let me go! My father is an important man! He is Mr. Frankenstein! He will punish you. You're not allowed to keep me."

"Frankenstein! So you belong to my enemy, the one I've sworn to get revenge on forever. You're going to be my first victim."

The child continued to struggle and called me names that filled my heart with despair. I silenced him by grabbing his throat, and in an instant, he lay lifeless at my feet.

I stared at my victim, feeling a surge of triumph and evil joy. Clapping my hands together, I proclaimed, "I too can bring devastation. My enemy is not invincible. This death will bring despair to him, and countless other miseries will torment and destroy him."

As I focused my gaze on the child, I noticed something shining on his chest. I took it; it was a portrait of a stunningly beautiful woman. Despite my cruel intentions, it softened my heart and captivated me. For a brief moment, I admired her dark eyes framed by long lashes and her lovely lips. But soon, my anger resurfaced. I remembered that I would forever be deprived of the joys that such beautiful beings could offer. And the woman whose likeness I looked upon would surely have changed her expression of divine kindness to one of disgust and terror if she had seen me.

Can you comprehend why such thoughts filled me with rage? I can only wonder why, at that moment, instead of expressing my emotions with shouts and agony, I didn't impulsively throw myself into the midst of humanity, risking my own life in an attempt to destroy them.

As overwhelmed as I was by these emotions, I left the area where I had committed the killing and searched for a more secluded place to hide. I entered a barn that seemed empty to me. There, I discovered a young woman sleeping on a bed of straw. Although she wasn't as beautiful as the woman in the portrait I held, she had a pleasant appearance and radiated the youth and health of her age. I couldn't help but think that she was one of those whose smiles could bring joy to everyone but me. In that moment, I leaned closer to her and whispered, "Wake up, my dearest. Your lover is here—someone who would give up their life just to see a look of affection in your eyes. My beloved, please awaken!"

The sleeper stirred, and a wave of fear coursed through me. What if she were to wake up, see me, and curse and accuse me of murder? Surely, that's how she would react if her eyes opened and she saw me. The thought was madness. It stirred the monster inside me. It wasn't me, but she who should suffer. I committed murder because I have been forever deprived of everything that she could have given me. Now, she must pay for it. The crime originated from her, so it should be her punishment! Thanks to the lessons I learned from Felix and the cruel laws of mankind, I had acquired the ability to cause harm. I leaned over her and carefully placed the portrait in one of the folds of her clothing. She stirred once more, and I quickly fled.

For a few days, I kept going back to the place where those events happened. Sometimes, I wanted to see you, but other times I was determined to leave the world and all its troubles forever. Finally, I made my way toward these mountains and I have been wandering through them ever since, consumed by a passionate desire that only you can fulfill. We cannot part until you promise to do what I ask. I am all alone and miserable; people refuse to be around me, but someone as disfigured and dreadful as myself would not reject me. My companion must be of the same kind and have the same imperfections. You must create this being.

CHAPTER

SEVENTEEN

 THE BEING FINISHED SPEAKING, and looked at me expectantly, waiting for a response. But I felt confused, overwhelmed, and couldn't gather my thoughts enough to fully understand what he was suggesting. He continued,

"You must make a female companion for me, someone with whom I can share the necessary emotions for my existence. Only you can do this, and I insist that you fulfill this request."

His later words reignited the anger that had faded as he recounted his peaceful life with the cottagers, and as he said this, I couldn't hold back the rage I felt inside.

"I refuse," I said firmly, "and no amount of torture will ever make me agree. You may make me the unhappiest person in the world, but I will never compromise my integrity. Should I create another creature like yourself, their shared wickedness could destroy the world. Leave now! I have given you my answer. You may torture me, but I will never give in."

 "You're wrong," the fiend replied. "Instead of making threats, I'm willing to reason with you. I am malicious because I am miserable. Doesn't everyone shun and hate me? You, my creator, would tear me

115

apart and celebrate. Remember that, and tell me why I should feel more pity for mankind than they feel for me? If you could push me into one of those ice crevasses and destroy the body you made, you wouldn't call it murder. Should I respect mankind when they treat me with contempt? Let them live with me, treating each other kindly. Instead of harming them, I would gladly help them, crying tears of gratitude if they accepted my generosity. But that's not possible; the differences in our human senses are insurmountable obstacles to our unity. Still, I will not submit as a powerless slave. I will seek revenge for the injustices I've suffered. If I cannot inspire love, I will inspire fear. And mainly towards you, my ultimate enemy as my creator, I swear to harbor an undying hatred. Be warned: I will work to bring about your destruction, and I won't stop until I leave your heart devastated, so that you'll curse the day of your birth."

A malicious rage consumed him as he said this; his face twisted into terrifying contortions too horrifying for any human to witness. But soon, he regained his composure and continued-

226   "I wanted to reason with you. This anger is harmful to me because you are the reason it has grown. If anyone showed kindness to me, I would return it many times over. I would make peace with all of humanity for the sake of that one person! But now I have impossible dreams of happiness. What I ask of you is fair and reasonable; I just want a companion who is as ugly as I am. It may not be much, but it would be enough for me. I know we would be outcasts from society, but that would only make us more connected to each other. Our lives may not be happy, but they would be peaceful and free from the misery I feel now. Oh, my creator, make me happy! Let me feel gratitude towards you for at least one act of kindness! Let me see that I can elicit sympathy from something in this world. Please don't deny my request!"

His words moved me. I trembled as I considered the potential consequences of granting his wish, but there was some truth in his argument. His story and his current emotions showed that he was capable of deep feelings. As his creator, didn't I owe him some measure of happiness? He noticed the change in my demeanor and continued speaking.

"If you agree, no one, including yourself, will ever see us again. I will travel to the vast wilderness of South America. I don't eat like humans do, I don't hunt and kill animals for food. Instead, I sustain myself with acorns and berries. My companion will be like me and will be satisfied with the same kind of food. We will make our bed with dried leaves, enjoying the warmth of the sun on our skin and the nourishment it provides. The picture I paint is one of peace and humanity. It should be clear to you that denying my request would only be an act of power and cruelty. Despite your previous heartlessness, I see compassion in your eyes now. Please, let me take advantage of this moment and persuade you to grant my fervent desire."

"You suggest," I replied, "escaping from human settlements and seeking refuge in the vast wilderness where only wild beasts will be your companions. How can you, who long for human love and sympathy, persist in this kind of exile? Eventually, you will return, seeking their kindness, only to be met with their disgust. Your destructive tendencies will resurface, and you will have a companion who will assist you in your destructive endeavors. This cannot happen. So, let us stop debating this point, for I cannot agree."

"How unpredictable your emotions are! Just moments ago, you were moved by my words, so why are you now closing yourself off to my complaints? I promise you, on the earth where I live and by the one who created me, that if you give me a companion, I will leave human civilization behind and live wherever fate takes me, even in the harshest of wilderness. My wicked desires will fade away, for I will find understanding! My life will pass peacefully, and in my final moments, I will not curse my creator."

His words had a strange impact on me. I felt sympathy for him and at times, a desire to comfort him. But when I looked at him, when I saw the repulsive figure that moved and spoke, my heart became sickened and my feelings transformed into horror and hatred. I tried to suppress these sensations, thinking that since I couldn't empathize with him, I had no right to deny him the small amount of happiness that I still had the ability to give.

"You promise," I said, "to be harmless. But haven't you already displayed a level of cruelty that should make me reasonably distrustful of you? Could this not be a deceit to further enhance your triumph by allowing for more opportunities for revenge?"

229   "What is happening here? I will not tolerate being deceived, and I expect an answer. If I have no connections or attachments, then I will be consumed by hatred and vice. Only the love of another can put an end to my wickedness and transform me into a person unknown to all. My wrongdoing is a result of the forced isolation that I despise, and my virtues will only emerge when I live in harmony with an equal. I will experience the emotions of a sensitive being and become part of the interconnected web of existence that currently excludes me."

I took a long pause to contemplate everything he had revealed and the arguments he had presented. I considered the initial display of virtues he had exhibited at the beginning of his existence as well as the experiences that followed. I also factored in his abilities and threats. I concluded that justice, both for him and my fellow human beings, required me to grant his request. So, I turned to him and said,

230   "I agree to your request, as long as you promise on a solemn oath to leave Europe and any other place near humans forever. Once I hand over a female companion, you must never be seen again," I replied.

"I swear," he exclaimed, "on the sun, the blue sky, and the fire of love that burns within me, that if you grant my plea, you will never see me again as long as they exist. Go back to your home and begin your task. I will anxiously watch its progress and when you are ready, I will appear."

Saying this, he abruptly left, perhaps afraid that my feelings towards him might change. I watched him descend the mountain with the swiftness of an eagle's flight, quickly disappearing among the waves of the icy sea.

231   His story had taken up the entire day, and now the sun was almost set as he left. I knew I should hurry down to the valley before darkness fell, but my heart felt heavy and my steps were slow. It was difficult to navigate the winding paths of the mountains and keep my balance as I walked. I was too preoccupied with the emotions stirred up by the events of the day. By the time I reached the halfway point, it was late at night. I sat down next to a fountain, with the stars occasionally shining through gaps in the passing clouds. The tall pine trees stood in front of me, and there were fallen trees scattered on the ground. It was a scene of great solemnity that made me think strange thoughts. I couldn't hold back my tears and in despair, I clasped my hands together and cried out, "Oh! Stars, clouds, and winds, you are all going to taunt me. If you truly have pity for me, take away my feelings and memories. Let me become nothing. But if you don't, then go away, go away, and leave me in darkness."

These thoughts were erratic and filled with misery. I can't properly explain how the constant twinkling of the stars made me feel weighed down, and how I anxiously listened to every gust of wind, fearing that it was a harsh and unpleasant wind that would devour me.

232   Morning came when I finally reached the village of Chamounix. I didn't stop to rest, but immediately headed back to Geneva. I couldn't find the words to express my feelings. They were so heavy, like a huge weight on my chest, and their intensity overwhelmed my suffering. So I returned home and walked into the house, joining my family. My tired and disheveled appearance alarmed them greatly, but I didn't answer their questions and hardly said a word. I felt like an outcast, as if I had no right to seek their sympathy, as if I could never be a part of their company again. Yet, despite all this, I loved them with an intense passion, and I decided to dedicate myself to a task I despised in order to protect them. The thought of this occupation consumed my every other thought, making everything else in life seem like a distant dream. Only that one thought felt real and alive to me.

CHAPTER

EIGHTEEN

233 WEEKS TURNED into months as I settled back into life in Geneva. Yet, I couldn't find the bravery to start my work again. I feared the wrath of the fiend who had been let down, but at the same time, I couldn't bring myself to face the distasteful task that had been assigned to me. Creating another female being required extensive research and study, something that would take me months to do. I had heard rumors of an English philosopher who had made some breakthroughs that could help me, and I briefly considered asking my father for permission to visit England for this purpose. However, I found excuses to put it off, feeling less urgency in completing the task. There had been a change in me; my health had improved and my spirits were lifted when I wasn't burdened by the memory of my ill-fated promise. My father noticed this change and sought ways to alleviate the remnants of my melancholy, which would occasionally return in fits of darkness, overshadowing the bright moments. During those moments, I sought solace in solitude, spending whole days alone in a little boat on the lake, observing the clouds and listening to the gentle waves, feeling empty and uninterested. But the fresh air and warm sun often brought me back to a state of calm,

120

and upon my return, I greeted my friends with a more genuine smile and a lighter heart.

After spending time alone and reflecting on my feelings, my father approached me with concern. He expressed his happiness in seeing me engage in activities that used to bring me joy and return to my former self. However, he also noticed that I still seemed unhappy and distant from our family. He couldn't understand the reason behind it and asked me to be honest with him, assuring me that keeping secrets would only bring more pain to all of us.

I felt my whole body shake as he began, and my father continued to speak. He admitted that he had always envisioned my marriage to Elizabeth, someone dear to our family, as a source of comfort and support in his old age. We had been close since childhood, studying together, and it seemed like we were a perfect match in temperament and interests. But he admitted that he may have been mistaken in his assumptions. He wondered if, in my eyes, Elizabeth was only a sister figure and if I had perhaps found someone else that I loved. He speculated that my inner turmoil stemmed from feeling obligated to Elizabeth due to a sense of honor, even if my heart belonged to another.

"Father, please do not worry. I deeply and sincerely love my cousin. Elizabeth is the only woman who has ever captured my heart and affection. My future and happiness rely entirely on the hope of marrying her."

"I am relieved to hear you express your feelings on this matter, Victor. If you truly feel this way, then we will undoubtedly be happy together, despite any current difficulties. However, it is the heaviness of your spirit that concerns me. I want to dispel this gloom that has taken such a strong hold on your mind. So please, tell me if you have any objections to a prompt marriage. We have been through unfortunate events lately, which have disrupted the peace and calmness that should accompany my old age and infirmities. You are younger, and even though you possess a sufficient wealth, I do not believe that an early marriage would interfere with any honorable and useful plans you may have for the future. Nonetheless, please understand that I do not wish to dictate your happiness, and a delay on your part would not cause me any serious uneasiness. Please interpret my words with honesty, and answer me candidly and confidently."

236   I listened to my father quietly, unable to respond for a while. Thoughts raced through my mind as I tried to come to a decision. Oh, the idea of marrying Elizabeth without delay filled me with horror and fear. I had made a solemn promise that I had not yet fulfilled, and I couldn't bring myself to break it. If I did, who knows what terrible consequences could befall me and my beloved family! How could I celebrate a wedding with this heavy burden still weighing me down, bending me to the ground? I had to honor my commitment and let the monster and his mate depart before I allowed myself to experience the joy of a union that promised peace.

237   I thought about what my father had said in silence and took some time to formulate a response. I had many thoughts swirling around in my head, trying to reach a conclusion. But the idea of marrying Elizabeth right away filled me with horror and fear. I had made a solemn promise that I couldn't break, for if I did, my family and I would surely suffer. How could I celebrate a wedding while burdened by such a heavy weight around my neck, keeping me down? I needed to fulfill my commitment and let the monster leave with his mate before allowing myself to enjoy the happiness that I hoped would come from our union.

238   I decided to share my true intentions with my father when he asked about my plans. I expressed a desire to visit England, but I didn't reveal the real reasons behind my request. Instead, I presented it in a way that wouldn't raise any suspicion. I spoke passionately about my longing for a change of scenery and the potential for enjoyment and entertainment that such a journey could bring. My father, who knew of my melancholy and understood its impact on me, eagerly agreed to my proposal. He hoped that the trip would help restore my well-being before I returned.

The length of my absence was left for me to decide. It was suggested that I should be away for a few months, or at most a year. To make sure I wouldn't be alone during my travels, my father took the initiative to arrange for my friend Clerval to accompany me in Strasbourg. Although this interrupted the solitude I craved to focus on my task, I couldn't deny that having my friend by my side would spare me from countless hours of lonely and tormenting reflection. In fact, I even took comfort in knowing that Henry's presence might serve as a barrier between me and the intrusion of my dreaded foe. If I were to be alone, wouldn't he occasionally force himself upon me to remind me of my duty or to observe its progress?

To England, that's where I had to go. The plan was for me to return and marry Elizabeth right away. My father, being older, didn't want any delays. As for me, there was one thing that kept me going through my horrible hardships - the thought of that day when I would finally be free and able to be with Elizabeth, forgetting everything that happened to me.

I started preparing for my journey, but there was a lingering fear that haunted me. While I was away, my friends would be completely unaware of the danger they were in, defenseless against the attacks of my enemy who would surely be furious with my departure. He had promised to follow me wherever I went, so would he come with me to England? The thought itself was terrifying, but it also brought some comfort in knowing that my friends might be safe. I was tormented by the possibility that the opposite could happen. However, during the time that I was under my creature's control, I allowed myself to be guided by the impulses of the moment, and right now, I strongly felt that the fiend would follow me and spare my family from his evil plans.

In late September, I left my home country once again. The decision to go on this journey was my own, and Elizabeth agreed to it. However, she was worried about the idea of me facing suffering and sadness while being away from her. She had been thoughtful enough to arrange for me to have a companion, Clerval, but sometimes a man fails to notice the little things that a woman pays attention to. She wanted to tell me to come back quickly, but her emotions were conflicting, and she could only bid me a tearful goodbye in silence.

I stepped into the carriage that would take me away, not caring where I was headed or what was happening around me. My only thought, and it filled me with bitter pain, was to make sure my chemical instruments were packed and brought along with me. Lost in gloomy thoughts, I traveled through many stunning and grand landscapes, but my eyes were fixed and unobservant. I could only think about my destination and the work that awaited me there.

241   After spending a few days aimlessly wandering, traveling many miles, I arrived at Strasburgh and waited for Clerval for two days. He finally arrived, and the difference between us was striking. He was fully present in each new experience, finding joy in the beauty of a sunset and happiness in the dawn of a new day. He enthusiastically pointed out the changing colors of the landscape and the patterns in the sky. "This is what it means to truly live," he exclaimed. "I am embracing life! But you, my dear Frankenstein, why are you so despairing and gloomy?" Honestly, my mind was consumed by dark thoughts, and I didn't even notice the evening star descending or the radiant sunrise reflecting on the Rhine. And, my friend, you would find much more enjoyment in reading Clerval's journal, as he observed the scenery with wonder and delight, rather than listening to my own reflections.

242   We had decided to travel down the Rhine in a boat from Strasburgh to Rotterdam, where we could then board a ship to London. During our journey, we passed many small islands covered in willow trees and saw several lovely towns. We stayed in Manheim for a day and, on the fifth day since leaving Strasburgh, we reached Mayence. The scenery along the Rhine below Mayence becomes much more picturesque. The river flows rapidly and winds its way between hills that are not tall but have beautiful shapes. We saw many ruins of castles perched on the edges of steep cliffs, surrounded by dark forests that were high and impossible to reach. This part of the Rhine

truly offers a diverse and varied landscape. In one area, you see rugged hills, crumbling castles overlooking dramatic cliffs, with the dark Rhine rushing underneath; and then, with a sudden turn of the land, you see flourishing vineyards, green sloping banks, a winding river, and towns bustling with people.

243 We traveled during the grape harvest and listened to the workers' song as we sailed down the river. Even though I was feeling down and constantly troubled by dark thoughts, I still found joy in the experience. I lay at the bottom of the boat and stared at the clear blue sky. It brought a sense of peace that I hadn't felt in a long time. And if I felt this way, imagine how Henry felt. He was transported to a magical land and experienced a happiness that few people get to feel. "I have seen," he said, "the most beautiful sights in my own country. I have been to the lakes of Lucerne and Uri, where the snowy mountains meet the water in a steep drop, casting dark shadows that would be gloomy if not for the bright islands that bring relief to the eye. I've seen the lake during a storm, when the winds whipped up whirlwinds of water, giving a taste of what a waterspout might be like in the open ocean. The waves fiercely crash against the base of the mountain, where a priest and his lover were buried by an avalanche, and some say their voices can still be heard in the night wind. I've seen the mountains of La Valais and the Pays de Vaud, but this place, Victor, is more enchanting than any of those wonders. The mountains of Switzerland are more majestic and strange, but there is a special charm to the banks of this beautiful river that I have never seen anywhere else. Look at that castle hanging over the precipice, and the one on the island, almost hidden by the lovely trees. And now, see those workers coming from their vineyards, and that village tucked away in the mountain's embrace. Oh, surely, the spirit that inhabits and protects this place understands mankind better than those who dwell in the icy glaciers or secluded peaks of our own mountains."

244 Clerval! My dear friend! I still find joy in recalling your words and praising you, for you truly deserve it. You were a person who seemed

to embody the very essence of nature's poetry. But even human connections were not enough to satisfy your curious mind. The beauty of the natural world, which others admire casually, brought you immense love and fascination.

"The sounding cataract
Haunted him like a passion: the tall rock,
The mountain, and the deep and gloomy wood,
Their colours and their forms, were then to him
An appetite; a feeling, and a love,
That had no need of a remoter charm,
By thought supplied, or any interest
Unborrow'd from the eye"

And where are you now? Has this gentle and beautiful soul vanished forever? Has this mind, filled with whimsical and grandiose ideas, which created a world that relied on its creator's existence - has this mind ceased to exist? Does it now only remain in my memories? No, that is not the case. Though your wonderfully crafted physical form has deteriorated, your spirit still visits and comforts your sorrowful friend.

245   Please excuse my outpouring of sadness. These words are only a small tribute to the exceptional value of Henry, but they bring some comfort to my heart, which is overwhelmed by the pain his memory brings. I will now continue with my story.

After leaving Cologne, we descended to the flat lands of Holland. The wind was against us and the river's current too weak, so we decided to travel the rest of the way by coach.

From this point on, our journey lacked the beauty of scenery. However, after a few days, we arrived in Rotterdam and from there we took a sea voyage to England. It was on a clear morning, in the last days of December, that I caught my first glimpse of the white cliffs of Britain. The banks of the Thames presented a new sight; they were flat but fertile, and each town held a historical significance. We saw Tilbury Fort and thought of the Spanish Armada, as well as

Gravesend, Woolwich, and Greenwich, places that I had even heard of in my homeland.

Finally, we caught sight of the numerous spires of London, with St. Paul's Cathedral towering above the rest, and the Tower of London, famous in English history.

CHAPTER
NINETEEN

246 WE STAYED in London for a while. Our main reason for being there was to gather information for a promise I had made. Clerval wanted to meet the talented and intelligent people who were prominent in the city at that time. However, for me, that was not of great importance. My main focus was on finding the knowledge I needed. I took advantage of the introduction letters I had brought with me, which were addressed to the most renowned natural philosophers.

If this journey had taken place during my days of studying and being happy, it would have brought me immense joy. But my life had been overshadowed by sadness, and I only sought out these people in order to gain insight into a subject that deeply interested me. Being around others was tedious for me. When I was alone, I could immerse myself in the wonders of the world around me and find comfort in Henry's voice. These brief moments offered me some respite from my despair. However, the presence of cheerful and lively faces only reminded me of the despair deep within my heart. I felt an unbridgeable gap between myself and others, a gap stained with the blood of William and Justine. Reflecting on the tragic events connected to those names caused me great anguish.

In Clerval, I saw a reflection of my past self. He was curious and eager to gain knowledge and experience. He had a long-standing goal to visit India, believing that his understanding of its languages and society could greatly contribute to European colonization and trade. He could only further his plans in Britain. He was always occupied, and the only thing that dampened his enjoyment was my sad state of mind. I tried to hide my feelings as best I could, so as not to deprive him of the natural joys that come with embarking on a new chapter in life. I frequently declined his invitations to join him, using some other excuse, just so I could be alone. Meanwhile, I began gathering the necessary materials for my new project, and each moment spent on it felt like the torment of individual droplets of water falling on my head. Every thought dedicated to it caused intense anguish, and every mention of it made my lips tremble and my heart race.

After spending a few months in London, we got a letter from someone in Scotland who had visited us in Geneva before. They talked about how beautiful their home country was and suggested that we should extend our journey to Perth, where they lived. Clerval was excited about accepting this invitation, and even though I usually didn't like being around people, I wanted to see the mountains and rivers again, and all the amazing things that Nature decorates her special places with.

We had arrived in England in October, and now it was February. So, we decided that in another month, we would start heading north. Instead of taking the main road to Edinburgh, our plan was to visit Windsor, Oxford, Matlock, and the Cumberland lakes. We wanted to finish this trip by the end of July. I packed up my science tools and the materials I had gathered, knowing that I would finish my work in some remote spot in the Scottish highlands.

On March 27th, we left London and spent a few days exploring the beautiful forest in Windsor. This was something new for us, who were used to mountains. The big oak trees, the abundance of wild animals, and the groups of majestic deer were all new and fascinating to us.

249   From there, we went to Oxford. When we arrived in this city, we couldn't help but think about the events that happened there more than one hundred and fifty years ago. This is where Charles I gathered his forces. Even when the whole nation abandoned him to support parliament and freedom, this city remained loyal to him. The memory of the unfortunate king and his companions - the likeable Falkland, the arrogant Goring, his queen, and his son - added a special interest to every part of the city that they might have lived in. The spirit of the past seemed to reside here, and we enjoyed following in its footsteps. If our emotional connection to this place wasn't enough, the city itself was beautiful enough to earn our admiration. The colleges are old and charming; the streets are almost grand; and the lovely Isis River, which flows alongside meadows of stunning greenery, spreads out to form a peaceful body of water. It reflects the magnificent towers, spires, and domes nestled among ancient trees.

250   I really enjoyed this scene, but my enjoyment was mixed with sadness from remembering the past and worrying about the future. I used to be so happy and content, and even when I felt bored, I could always find solace in the beauty of nature or the great accomplishments of humanity. But now, I feel like a withered tree, ruined by a terrible event that has left me feeling hopeless and miserable. I know that I'll soon become a pitiful sight, both to others and to myself.

We spent a long time in Oxford, exploring the surrounding areas and trying to find every place connected to the most exciting time in English history. Our adventures often took longer than expected because there were so many interesting things to see. We went to Hampden's tomb and the field where he died, both of which reminded me of the noble ideals of liberty and sacrifice. For a moment, I felt uplifted and free, but then I remembered the pain I was carrying and sank back into hopelessness.

251   We left Oxford reluctantly and traveled to Matlock, our next destination. The countryside near this village resembled the scenery of Switzerland, although on a smaller scale. However, I couldn't help

but notice that the green hills lacked the majestic white Alps that I was accustomed to seeing in my homeland. We explored the fascinating cave and the quaint collections of natural history, which reminded me of similar exhibits in Servox and Chamounix. The mention of Chamounix brought back terrifying memories, so I quickly left Matlock, hoping to escape that dreadful scene.

Continuing our journey north from Derby, we spent two months in Cumberland and Westmorland. I almost felt as if I were amongst the mountains of Switzerland. The patches of snow lingering on the northern slopes, the picturesque lakes, and the sounds of rushing streams all felt familiar and comforting to me. During our time there, we made some acquaintances who managed to bring a hint of happiness into my life. Clerval, in particular, thrived in the company of talented individuals. He discovered hidden abilities within himself that he never knew existed when surrounded by those of lesser capabilities. "I could live here forever," he said to me. "Among these mountains, I would hardly miss Switzerland and the Rhine."

However, he discovered that being a traveler can be both joyful and challenging. It requires constantly being on the move, never truly able to relax and fully enjoy one's surroundings. Just as he starts to find comfort and happiness in a particular place, he is compelled to leave it in search of something new. This cycle repeats itself, with each new discovery capturing his attention, only to be left behind for yet another unfamiliar experience.

We hadn't spent much time exploring the lakes of Cumberland and Westmorland, or getting to know some of the locals, when it was time for us to meet up with our friend from Scotland and continue our travels. Personally, I wasn't too upset about leaving. I had been neglecting my promise for a while now, and I was afraid that my failure would anger the demon. I worried that he might stay in Switzerland and seek revenge on my family. This thought haunted me and kept me from finding any peace or rest. I anxiously awaited my letters, fearing any delay would bring me misery and countless fears. And when they finally arrived, with Elizabeth or my father's name on the envelope, I was afraid to read them and find out my fate. Sometimes I was convinced that the demon was pursuing me, and that he might speed up my negligence by harming my friend. Whenever these thoughts consumed me, I refused to leave Henry's side, following him closely to protect him from the imaginary wrath of his assailant. I felt as though I had committed a grave crime, even though I was innocent. But I had brought upon myself a terrible curse, just as real as the punishment for a wrongdoing.

254 With tired eyes and a weary mind, I made my way to Edinburgh. Despite my own feelings of exhaustion, it was a city that could captivate even the most unfortunate soul. However, Clerval wasn't as enamored with it as he had been with Oxford. The ancient history of Oxford held more charm for him. But the orderly and picturesque new town of Edinburgh, with its enchanting castle, and the surrounding natural beauty of Arthur's Seat, St. Bernard's Well, and the Pentland Hills, brought him joy and wonder. As for me, I was eager to reach the end of my journey.

After a week, we departed from Edinburgh. Our path took us through Coupar, St. Andrew's, and along the banks of the Tay, until we reached Perth where our friend was waiting for us. However, I was in no mood to socialize, to laugh and converse with strangers, or to show the expected cheerfulness of a guest. I confided in Clerval, expressing my desire to explore Scotland on my own. I told him, "Enjoy yourself and let this be our meeting point. I might be away for a month or two, so please respect my need for solitude. When I return, I hope to have a lighter heart that matches your own."

255 Henry tried to convince me otherwise, but realizing my determination, he stopped arguing. He asked me to write to him often. He urged me to return quickly so that he could feel at home again.

After saying goodbye to my friend, I decided to visit a remote area of Scotland to complete my work in peace. I was certain that the monster was following me and would reveal himself once I had finished, expecting me to be his companion.

With this plan in mind, I traveled through the northern highlands and chose one of the farthest Orkney Islands as my working place. It was a fitting location for my task, as it was nothing more than a rocky formation constantly battered by the waves. The land was barren and only provided enough pasture for a few malnourished cows. The residents of this place, a group of five individuals, had emaciated bodies that showed signs of their meager diet. They relied on the mainland, which was approximately five miles away, for vegetables, bread, and even fresh water.

On the entire island, there were only three poor huts, and one of them was empty when I arrived. I rented it. It had only two rooms, which were extremely run-down. The roof was falling apart, the walls were bare, and the door was broken. I had it fixed, bought some furniture, and moved in; an event that would have probably surprised the villagers if they weren't so numbed by poverty and hardship. As it was, I lived there unnoticed and undisturbed, barely thanked for the small amount of food and clothes I gave; suffering can dull even the most basic human feelings.

In this quiet place, I spent my mornings working. But in the evenings, when the weather was good, I went for walks on the rocky beach, listening to the sound of the waves crashing at my feet. It was a repetitive yet ever-changing sight. I thought of Switzerland; it was completely different from this empty and frightening landscape. In Switzerland, the hills are covered in vineyards and the houses are scattered across the plains. The beautiful lakes reflect a calm, blue sky; and even when they're stirred up by the wind, their noise is nothing compared to the roaring of the massive ocean.

When I first arrived, I divided my time between various tasks. However, as I continued my work, it became more and more unpleasant. There were days when I couldn't bring myself to enter my laboratory, and other times when I would toil day and night to finish what I had started. The process itself was absolutely repulsive. At the beginning, I was so consumed by my goal that I didn't even realize the horror of my actions. My mind was solely focused on completing my work, and I shut out any feelings of dread. But now, I approached it with a clear mind, and my heart would often become sickened by what my hands were doing.

Being in this situation, engaged in such a loathsome task, and isolated in a place where nothing could distract me from what I was doing, my mood started to fluctuate. I became restless and anxious. I was afraid of encountering my tormentor at any moment. Sometimes I would sit with my eyes fixed on the ground, afraid to look up, in case I saw the very thing I dreaded the most. I was afraid to be alone, as I thought he might come to claim me.

In the meantime, I continued to work, and my progress was already quite significant. I looked forward to completing it with a combination of excitement and fear. There was a part of me that was too afraid to question my eager hope, but at the same time, I had a sense of impending trouble that made me feel sick inside.

TWENTY

ONE EVENING, I sat in my laboratory. The sun had gone down and the moon was rising from the sea. The dim light made it difficult to continue my work, so I hesitated, unsure if I should stop for the night or push through and finish. While I pondered, I started to reflect on the consequences of my actions. Three years ago, I was in a similar situation, creating a monster whose brutality had devastated me and left me consumed by regret. Now, I was about to bring another being into existence. While the original monster had vowed to stay away from humanity and live in isolation, there was no such guarantee from this new being. Being capable of thinking and reasoning, it might reject the agreement made before its creation. It could even despise the existing monster due to its own grotesque appearance, especially if presented in a female form. Perhaps it would be attracted to the beauty of humans, abandoning the monster and leaving it alone once again. This desertion might further enrage the monster, feeling the sting of rejection from its own kind.

Even if they were to leave Europe and live in the deserts of the new world, one of the consequences of the creature's thirst for companionship would be the birth of children, creating a race of devils that could pose a threat to the existence of humanity. Did I have the right to subject future generations to this curse just for my own benefit? I had previously been swayed by the creature's arguments and frightened by his evil threats, but now, for the first time, the wickedness of my promise struck me. I shuddered at the thought that people in the future might curse me as their tormentor, blaming my selfishness for potentially endangering the entire human race.

I trembled with fear and my heart sank when I looked up and saw the creature at the window, illuminated by the moonlight. A disturbing grin twisted his lips as he stared at me, observing me as I carried out the task he had given me. Yes, he had been following me during my travels, lingering in forests, hiding in caves, and seeking refuge in vast, uninhabited plains. Now, he had come to witness my progress and demand that I fulfill my promise.

I watched his face, filled with pure evil and deceit. Thoughts of my foolish promise to create another like him flooded my mind, driving me to a state of madness. Overwhelmed with anger, I violently tore apart the abomination I was working on. The monster witnessed me destroying its potential for happiness, and in a fit of despair and vengeance, let out a chilling howl and vanished.

Leaving the room, I locked the door and made a solemn promise to myself that I would never continue my experiments. With trembling steps, I retreated to my own chamber. I was completely alone, with no one to alleviate the darkness or free me from the suffocating weight of my tormenting thoughts.

Hours went by as I stood by my window, staring out at the calm sea. The waters were motionless, as if the winds themselves had fallen silent, and the entire world slumbered under the watchful gaze of the peaceful moon. Only a few fishing boats dotted the surface of the water, and every so often, I caught snippets of voices as the fishermen called out to one another. The silence was so profound that I could feel it, though I wasn't fully aware of its depth, until my attention was abruptly seized by the sound of oars paddling near the shore and the arrival of a person right by my house.

A few minutes later, I heard the sound of my door creaking, as if someone was trying to open it quietly. I was filled with fear from head to toe. I had a feeling of who it might be and wanted to wake up one of the villagers who lived nearby, but I felt completely helpless, like in a terrifying dream where you try to escape danger but can't move.

Soon, I heard footsteps approaching along the hallway. The door opened and the person I feared appeared. He closed the door behind him and came towards me, speaking in a suppressed voice.

"You have destroyed the project you started. What are your intentions now? Do you dare to break your promise? I have endured hardship and misery. I followed you from Switzerland; I traveled through the riverside islands and over the hills of the Rhine. I spent many months in the English moors and the Scottish wilderness. I endured endless fatigue, cold, and hunger. Do you dare to crush my hopes?"

"Go away! I am breaking my promise. I will never create another being like you, with the same ugliness and wickedness."

"Slave, I tried to reason with you before, but you have proven yourself unworthy of my kindness. Remember that I have power. You may think you are miserable, but I can make you so unhappy that you will hate the daylight. You are my creator, but I am your master. Obey me!"

"The time for my indecision has passed, and now is the moment of your control. Your threats cannot persuade me to commit an evil act; instead, they strengthen my decision not to create you a companion in wickedness. Will I, with a clear mind, release onto the world a monster who finds delight in death and suffering? Begone! I am steadfast, and your words will only make my anger worse."

The creature recognized my determination from my expression and clenched his teeth in furious frustration. "Shall every man," he cried, "find a wife for his heart, and every animal have its mate, while I remain alone? I had feelings of affection, but they were met with hatred and disdain. Man! You may hate, but be careful! Your hours will be filled with dread and misery, and soon the punishment will come that will rob you of happiness forever. Will you be content while I wallow in my intense misery? You may extinguish my other emotions, but revenge remains—revenge, now dearer to me than light or food! I may die, but first, you, my oppressor and tormentor, will curse the sun that looks upon your suffering. Be warned, for I am fearless, and thus, powerful. I will observe you like a cunning snake, ready to strike with venom. Man, you will regret the harm you have inflicted."

"Devil, stop! Do not pollute the air with these malicious words. I have stated my decision to you, and I am not a coward who will yield to mere words. Leave me; I am unyielding."

"Alright then. I'm leaving, but just remember, I'll be there on your wedding night."

I quickly stood up and shouted, "You villain! Before you seal my fate, make sure you're safe too."

I tried to grab him, but he slipped away and left the house in a hurry. In a matter of moments, I saw him in his boat, zooming across the water, and soon vanishing into the waves.

Everything was quiet again, but his words echoed in my mind. I felt burning anger, wanting to chase after the murderer of my happiness and throw him into the ocean. I paced back and forth in my room, feeling restless and disturbed, as my imagination tortured and haunted me. Why hadn't I gone after him and fought him to the death? Instead, I had let him escape, heading towards the mainland. I trembled at the thought of who might be his next target, as he thirsted for revenge. And then I remembered his words - "I will be with you on your wedding night." That was the time when my destiny would be fulfilled. I would die in that hour, satisfying and ending his cruel intentions. I didn't feel fear at the prospect, but when I thought about my beloved Elizabeth - her tears and everlasting sadness upon discovering her lover cruelly taken away from her - tears, the first I had cried in months, welled up in my eyes. I vowed not to surrender to my enemy without a bitter fight.

The night went by, and the sun rose over the ocean. I started to feel somewhat calmer, although it was hard to call it calmness when my rage had turned into despair. I left the house, the terrible place where the argument happened last night, and walked along the beach. I felt like the sea was a barrier, keeping me separate from other people. At that moment, I even wished it was true. I wanted to spend my life on that lonely rock, although it would be dull and full of sadness, at least I wouldn't be hit by sudden waves of misery. If I returned, it would be to be sacrificed or to witness the death of the ones I loved at the hands of the monster I created.

I wandered around the island like a restless ghost, separated from everything I cared about, and miserable because of it. When it was noon and the sun was high in the sky, I laid down on the grass and fell into a deep sleep. I had been awake for the whole night, my nerves were on edge, and my eyes were tired from crying and unhappiness. The sleep that overcame me gave me some relief, and when I woke up, I felt like I was a part of humanity once again. I started to think more calmly about what had happened, but the words of the fiend still echoed in my ears like a death bell. They seemed like a dream, but also very real and oppressive.

As the sun began to set, I remained seated on the shore, devouring an oaten cake to satisfy my starving hunger. Suddenly, a fishing boat arrived and docked near me. One of the men handed me a package containing letters from Geneva, including one from Clerval pleading with me to join him. He explained that he was wasting his time where he was and that his friends in London were urging him to return so they could finalize plans for his Indian venture. He couldn't delay his departure any longer, and he believed his journey to London would be followed by a longer voyage sooner than he expected. He begged me to leave my lonely island and meet him in Perth so that we could travel together toward the south. Reading this letter brought me back to life, and I made up my mind to leave the island within two days.

Before I left, there was a task I had to do that made me feel uneasy just thinking about it: I needed to pack up my chemical tools. To do that, I had to go into the room where I had done my terrible work, and I had to touch those tools that made me sick just to look at them. The next morning, at sunrise, I gathered up enough courage to unlock the door to my laboratory. The remains of the half-finished creature I had destroyed were scattered on the floor, and it felt like I had hurt a living person. I took a moment to compose myself, and then went into the room. With a trembling hand, I moved the tools out of the room. But I realized that I shouldn't leave behind any evidence of what I had done, because it would frighten and make the villagers suspicious. So, I put the tools into a basket along with a lot of stones, and decided to throw them into the sea that night. In the meantime, I sat on the beach, cleaning and organizing my chemical equipment.

267   The change in my emotions since the night the creature appeared was truly remarkable. I used to view my promise with a sense of deep hopelessness, feeling obligated to fulfill it regardless of the consequences. However, something shifted within me, and it was as if a cloud had been lifted from my vision, allowing me to see clearly for the first time. The thought of continuing my experiments never crossed my mind. The warning I had received weighed heavily on my thoughts, although I didn't consider the possibility that I could prevent it through my own actions. I had firmly made up my mind that creating another creature like the one I had previously made would be a selfish and utterly abhorrent act. Any thoughts that could lead to a different decision were forcefully banished from my mind.

268   Around two or three in the morning, the moon began to rise. I decided to take my basket and hop into a small boat and sail about four miles away from the shore. The area was completely deserted, and while a few boats were making their way back to land, I purposely steered away from them. It felt as though I was about to commit a terrible crime, so I anxiously avoided any interactions with other people. At one point, the previously clear moon was suddenly covered by a thick cloud. I took advantage of the darkness and

quickly tossed my basket into the sea. I listened to the satisfying sound of it sinking and then swiftly sailed away from the spot. The sky became cloudy, but the air was fresh, even though a chilly breeze was blowing in from the northeast. It revitalized me and filled me with pleasant sensations, which led me to decide to prolong my stay on the water. I set the rudder in a straight direction and laid down at the bottom of the boat. The clouds obscured the moon, making everything dark and the only sound I heard was the boat gliding through the waves. The soothing sound lulled me to sleep, and before I knew it, I was soundly asleep.

269   I do not know how long I remained in this situation, but when I awoke I found that the sun had already risen. The wind was high and drifted me from my intended path. I endeavoured to change my course, but quickly found that, if I again made the attempt, the boat would be instantly filled with water. Thus situated, my only resource was to drive before the wind. I confess that I felt a few sensations of terror. I had no compass with me and I had already been out many hours, and felt the torment of a burning thirst, a prelude to my other sufferings. I looked on the heavens, which were covered by clouds that flew before the wind, only to be replaced by others. I looked upon the sea, it was to be my grave. "Fiend," I exclaimed, "your task is already fulfilled!" I thought of Elizabeth, of my father, and of Clerval; all left behind, on whom the monster might satisfy his sanguinary and merciless passions. This idea plunged me into a reverie, so despairing and frightful, that even now, when the scene is on the point of closing before me for ever, I shudder to reflect on it.

270   AFTER SOME TIME HAD PASSED, as the sun lowered in the sky, the wind gradually calmed down to a gentle breeze, and the sea became calm. However, there was still a large swell in the water. I felt sick and weak, struggling to hold onto the rudder. Suddenly, I noticed a line of land to the south.

    Despite my exhaustion and the hours of fear and uncertainty I had endured, the certainty of life filled my heart with overwhelming joy, bringing tears to my eyes.

It's remarkable how our emotions can change so quickly, and how even in the depths of misery, we have an instinctual love for life. I used part of my clothing to create another sail and eagerly steered towards the land. It looked rugged and rocky from a distance, but as I got closer, I could see signs of human cultivation. I spotted boats near the shore and felt a sense of relief at being back in the presence of civilization. I carefully followed the twists and turns of the coastline and eventually spotted a church tower emerging from behind a small peninsula. Since I was incredibly weak, I decided to head directly towards the town, hoping to find nourishment there. Thankfully, I had some money on me. As I rounded the peninsula, I discovered a small, tidy town with a welcoming harbor. I entered the harbor, my heart filled with joy at my unexpected escape.

As I worked on securing the boat and arranging the sails, a group of people gathered around me. They appeared surprised by my presence, but instead of offering help, they whispered among themselves in a way that could have made me slightly uneasy under different circumstances. However, at that moment, I simply noticed that they were speaking English. So, I decided to address them in the same language. "Excuse me, my good friends," I said, "could you please tell me the name of this town and where I am?"

"You'll find out soon enough," replied a man with a rough, hoarse voice. "You might not find this place to be great, but you also won't have much choice."

I was extremely surprised to receive such a rude response from a stranger. "Why are you answering me so harshly?" I retorted. "Surely it is not customary for English people to welcome strangers so inhospitably."

"I don't know," said the man, "what the English are accustomed to, but it is the Irish way to despise scoundrels."

While this strange conversation continued, I noticed more and more people gathering around. Their faces showed a mix of curiosity and anger, which both annoyed and worried me. I asked for directions to the inn, but no one answered. So, I started walking ahead, and the crowd followed and surrounded me. Then, a man with a menacing look tapped me on the shoulder and said, "Come, Sir, you must come with me to Mr. Kirwin's. You need to explain yourself."

"Who is Mr. Kirwin? Why do I have to explain myself? Isn't this a free country?"

"Yes, sir, it is free for honest people. Mr. Kirwin is a magistrate, and you need to explain what happened to a man who was found murdered here last night."

His response startled me, but I quickly regained my composure. I was innocent, and that could easily be proven. So, I followed the man in silence and was led to one of the nicest houses in town. I was exhausted and hungry, but since I was surrounded by a crowd, I knew I had to gather all my strength. I couldn't let any signs of physical tiredness be mistaken for fear or guilt. Little did I know then the tragedy that was about to unfold, shattering all my hopes of escaping shame or death.

I need to take a break here. It takes a lot of bravery to remember and explain the horrifying events that are about to come to mind.

TWENTY-ONE

273   I WAS SOON INTRODUCED into the presence of the magistrate, an old benevolent man, with calm and mild manners. He looked upon me, however, with some degree of severity. Then, turning towards my conductors, he asked who appeared as witnesses on this occasion.

274   Around six men stepped forward, and one of them was chosen by the magistrate. He testified that he had gone fishing the previous night with his son and brother-in-law, Daniel Nugent. At around ten o'clock, they noticed a strong northerly gust of wind picking up, so they decided to head back to the port. It was a very dark night since the moon hadn't risen yet. Instead of landing at the harbor, they docked at a creek about two miles away, as they usually did. The witness led the way, carrying some of the fishing equipment, while his companions followed at a distance. As he walked along the sandy beach, he tripped over something and fell to the ground. His companions hurried over to help, and using the light from their lantern, they discovered that he had fallen on the body of a man who appeared lifeless. Initially, they assumed it was the body of someone who had drowned and washed ashore, but upon closer inspection, they noticed that the clothes were dry and the body wasn't cold yet.

They immediately took the body to the cottage of an elderly woman nearby and tried, unsuccessfully, to revive him. The deceased was a young man of about twenty-five, seemingly strangled, as the only signs of harm were the finger marks encircling his neck.

The beginning of that statement didn't really catch my attention, but when they mentioned the mark on the neck, it reminded me of my brother's murder. It made me feel really uneasy and I started shaking. I had to lean on a chair to steady myself. The magistrate noticed my reaction and probably thought I was acting suspiciously.

The son confirmed what his father said. But then Daniel Nugent took the stand and swore that right before his friend fell, he saw a boat with only one person in it, not far from the shore. He said that, from the few stars he could see, it looked like the same boat I had just come in on.

A woman who lived near the beach stated that she was standing at her cottage door, waiting for the fishermen to come back, about an hour before she heard that they found the body. She said she saw a boat with only one person in it, heading out from where the body was later found.

Another woman confirmed what the fishermen said about bringing the body into her house. She said it wasn't cold. They put it in a bed and tried to revive it. Daniel went to town to get a doctor, but it was clear that there was no life left in the person.

A few other men were questioned about my arrival. They agreed that due to the strong north wind that had come up during the night, it was likely that I had been sailing around for many hours and had to return almost to the same place from where I had left. Furthermore, they noted that it seemed like I had brought the body from somewhere else, and it was possible that since I didn't appear to be familiar with the shore, I might have sailed into the harbor unaware of the distance between it and the town where I had left the corpse.

Upon hearing this testimony, Mr. Kirwin requested that I be taken to the room where the body was being prepared for burial, to observe my reaction upon seeing it. This idea probably came to him because of my extreme distress when the details of the murder were discussed. Therefore, the magistrate and several others escorted me to the inn. I couldn't help but notice the strange coincidences that had occurred during this eventful night. However, since I knew that I had been talking to various people on the island I had been living on around the time the body was found, I felt completely calm about the consequences of the situation.

277   I walked into the room where the dead body was, and they guided me to the coffin. How can I explain how I felt when I saw it? I still feel scared and horrified when I think about that moment. The investigation, with the magistrate and the people watching, felt like a blur in my memory as soon as I saw the lifeless body of Henry Clerval in front of me. I couldn't breathe, and I threw myself onto the body, saying, "Did my evil plans also take away your life, my dear Henry? I have already killed two people, and there are more victims to come. But you, Clerval, my friend, my helper..."

I couldn't handle the pain anymore, and I was carried out of the room while having strong convulsions.

After that, I got a fever. I was near death for two months: I later heard that I said terrible things in my feverish state. I called myself the murderer of William, of Justine, and of Clerval. Sometimes I begged my caretakers to help me get rid of the monster tormenting me, and other times I felt its fingers tightening around my neck and I screamed in pain and terror. Luckily, since I was speaking my own language, only Mr. Kirwin understood me, but my gestures and cries frightened everyone else who was there.

278   Why didn't I die? I was more miserable than anyone had ever been before. Why didn't I just forget everything and find peace? Death takes away many young children, the only hope for their loving parents. How many young couples and lovers have gone from being healthy and full of hope one day, to becoming food for worms and decaying in a tomb the next? What was I made of, that I could endure so many painful experiences that constantly brought back the torture, like a wheel that never stops turning?

But I wasn't meant to die. And after two months, I found myself waking up from a horrible dream, in a prison. I was lying on a terrible bed, surrounded by guards, keys, locks, and all the sad things that come with being in a dungeon. I remember it was morning when I finally understood what was happening. I had forgotten the details of what had occurred, and only felt as if a great misfortune had suddenly come over me. But when I looked around and saw the barred windows and the terrible condition of the room I was in, all the memories flooded back, and I let out a deep, painful groan.

This noise disturbed an old woman who was sleeping in a chair next to me. She was a hired nurse, the wife of one of the guards, and her face revealed all the negative qualities often seen in people of that class. Her features were harsh and rude, like those of someone accustomed to witnessing misery without any sympathy. Her tone showed complete indifference as she spoke to me in English, and her voice struck me as one I had heard during my suffering:

"Are you feeling better now, sir?" she asked.

I replied with a weak voice in the same language, "I believe I am. But if everything that happened is true, if I didn't dream it all, then I am sorry that I am still alive to experience this misery and horror."

"Well," the old woman responded, "if you're talking about the gentleman you murdered, I think it would be better for you if you were dead. I imagine things won't go well for you! But that's none of my concern. I am here to nurse you and help you get better. I do my duty with a clear conscience. It would be good if everyone did the same."

I turned away from the woman in disgust. How could she speak so heartlessly to someone who had just been saved from the brink of death? But I felt weak and unable to reflect on everything that had happened. My entire life seemed like a dream to me. I sometimes doubted that it was all true because it never felt as real as it should have.

As the pictures that appeared in front of me became clearer, I grew restless; a darkness surrounded me: there was no one nearby to calm me with a kind and loving voice; no comforting hand to support me. The doctor came and prescribed medicine, and the old woman prepared it for me; but the doctor showed no care in his actions, and the old woman's face displayed a cruel expression. Who could possibly care about the fate of a murderer, except for the executioner who would collect their fee?

These were my initial thoughts, but I soon discovered that Mr. Kirwin had shown me great kindness. He had arranged for the best room in the prison to be prepared for me (although even the best room was miserable); and it was he who had arranged for a doctor and a nurse. It's true that he didn't visit me often; for, although he sincerely wanted to alleviate the suffering of every human being, he did not want to witness the agonizing and delusional ramblings of a murderer. Therefore, he would occasionally come to ensure that I was not being neglected; but his visits were short and infrequent.

While I was slowly getting better, I sat in a chair with my eyes half open and pale cheeks that looked like death. I was overwhelmed by sadness and despair, often thinking that death would be preferable to staying in a world filled with misery. I even considered confessing my guilt and accepting the punishment, feeling less innocent than poor Justine. These were my thoughts when Mr. Kirwin entered my room. His face showed sympathy and compassion. He pulled a chair close to mine and spoke to me in French.

"I understand that this place is very disturbing for you. Is there anything I can do to make you more comfortable?"

"Thank you, but nothing you mentioned matters to me. There is no comfort in the whole world that I am capable of receiving."

"I know that the sympathy of a stranger can only bring little relief to someone burdened by such a strange misfortune. But I hope that you will soon leave this sad place, as surely evidence can be found to prove your innocence."

"That is my least concern. Through a series of strange events, I have become the most miserable person alive. Persecuted and tortured as I am, can death be any worse for me?"

"Nothing could be more unfortunate and distressing than the strange series of events that have recently taken place. You were unexpectedly stranded on this hospitable shore, only to be immediately arrested and accused of murder. The first thing you saw upon arriving was the lifeless body of your friend, a victim of a baffling crime that seemed to have been deliberately placed in your path by some malevolent force."

As Mr. Kirwin spoke, I couldn't help but be both shaken by the memories of my suffering and surprised by his apparent knowledge of my situation. My expression must have revealed my astonishment, because Mr. Kirwin quickly added,

"As soon as you fell ill, all the belongings you had on you were given to me. I searched through them in the hopes of finding some clue that would allow me to inform your family about your misfortune and illness. Among the letters I found, one was from your father. Without hesitation, I wrote to Geneva. It has been almost two months since I sent that letter. But, I can see that you are unwell; even now, you're trembling. You should avoid any form of distress."

"This state of uncertainty is far worse than any dreadful event. Please, tell me what new tragedy has occurred, and whose death I am now mourning."

"Your family is perfectly fine," Mr. Kirwin responded gently. "In fact, someone, a friend, has come to visit you."

I don't know how I came to think of it, but suddenly the idea entered my mind that the killer had come to mock my suffering and taunt me with Clerval's death, as a new way to make me comply with their evil desires. I covered my eyes with my hand and cried out in agony—

"Oh! Get him away! I can't bear to see him; please, don't let him come in!"

Mr. Kirwin looked at me with a troubled expression. He couldn't help but think that my outburst was a sign of my guilt, and he responded in a rather stern tone—

"Young man, I would have expected that you would welcome the presence of your father instead of showing such strong aversion."

"My father!" I exclaimed, my face and body going from anguish to joy. "Has my father really come? How kind, how very kind! But where is he? Why isn't he hurrying to see me?"

My change in demeanor surprised and pleased the magistrate; perhaps he thought that my previous outcry was just a momentary lapse due to my illness. Instantly, he returned to his previous kindness. He stood up, left the room with my nurse, and in a moment, my father entered.

At that moment, nothing could have brought me greater joy than the arrival of my father. I reached out my hand to him and asked—

"Are you safe then—and Elizabeth—and Ernest?"

My father comforted me by assuring me that my family was safe and well. He tried to lift my spirits by talking about the things that were dear to my heart, but he soon realized that a prison is not a place for happiness. "What a terrible place you are in, my son!" he said sadly, looking at the barred windows and the miserable room. "You went on a journey to find joy, but it seems that misfortune follows you. And poor Clerval—"

Hearing the name of my friend, who was tragically murdered, was too much for me to bear in my weakened state. I wept.

"Yes, father," I replied. "I am destined for something dreadful, and I must live to fulfill it. Otherwise, I would have died with Henry in his coffin."

We were not allowed to talk for long since my health was fragile and needed to be taken care of. Mr. Kirwin entered and insisted that I shouldn't exert myself too much. But the sight of my father was like seeing my guardian angel, and my health slowly began to improve.

After my illness passed, I was consumed by a deep and dark sadness that nothing could dispel. The vision of Clerval's lifeless and dreadful body haunted me constantly. The intensity of these thoughts caused my friends to fear that I might suffer a dangerous setback. Why, I wondered, did I have to endure such a wretched and despised existence? It must be because I have a destiny to fulfill, which is nearing its end. Death will soon come to extinguish these agonizing throbs, releasing me from the overwhelming weight of pain that drags me down. And in carrying out justice, I will finally find rest. Death seemed far away at that time, despite my constant desire for its arrival. I would often sit for hours, completely still and silent, yearning for a great upheaval that could bury both me and my tormentor.

The time for the trial was approaching. I had already spent three months in prison and, despite still being weak and at risk of getting sick again, I had to travel a hundred miles to the county-town where the court was held. Mr. Kirwin took charge of finding witnesses and organizing my defense. Luckily, I didn't have to face the disgrace of appearing in public as a criminal, since the case did not go before the court that decides on life and death. The grand jury dismissed the charges when it was proven that I was on the Orkney Islands when my friend's body was discovered. Two weeks after being moved, I was released from prison.

My father was overjoyed to see me freed from the burden of a criminal accusation and to have me back in our homeland. But I couldn't share in his happiness, as the walls of a dungeon were just as repulsive to me as the walls of a palace. The taste of life had forever turned bitter for me. Even though the sun shone on me, like it did on those who were happy and carefree, all I saw around me was a thick and terrifying darkness, with no light except for the glim-mering of two eyes that stared at me. Sometimes, they were the tender and soulful eyes of my late friend Henry, his dark eyes almost obscured by his eyelids and the long black lashes that framed them. Other times, they were the watery and clouded eyes of the monster, the same eyes I first saw in my room in Ingolstadt.

My father tried to make me feel love and happiness again. He talked about our upcoming visit to Geneva and about my cousins, Elizabeth and Ernest. But these words only made me groan deeply. Sometimes, I did feel a desire for happiness. I would think with sad pleasure about my beloved cousin or long to see the beautiful blue lake and fast-moving Rhone river that were so precious to me in my early childhood. But most of the time, I felt numb, and being in a prison felt just as welcoming as being in the most heavenly place in nature. These moments of feeling were rarely interrupted, except by episodes of intense pain and despair. In those moments, I often wanted to end the life that I hated, and it took constant care and watchfulness to stop me from doing something horrible.

288   There was one important task that I had to fulfill, despite my own despair. I needed to go back to Geneva as soon as possible, in order to protect the lives of my beloved ones. I also had to find the murderer. I hoped that I would have the courage and determination to end the existence of this monstrous individual, who I believed was even more monstrous than the soulless being he had become. Despite my father's concerns about my ability to handle the strenuous journey, he still wished to postpone our departure. I had become a broken, feeble version of myself – a mere shadow. I was physically depleted, reduced to a skeleton, and afflicted with constant fever that consumed my frail body day and night.

289   Even though I strongly urged my father to leave Ireland with impatience and concern, he decided it would be best to acquiesce. We secured our passage on a ship heading to Havre-de-Grace, and we set sail with a favorable wind, leaving the shores of Ireland behind. It was midnight, and I found myself lying on the deck, gazing up at the stars and listening to the crash of the waves. I greeted the darkness that concealed Ireland from my view, and my heart raced with excitement when I realized that soon I would be reunited with my loved ones in Geneva. The past seemed like a horrifying nightmare to me. Yet everything around me reminded me too vividly that my experiences were no mere figment of my imagination. Clerval, my dear friend and faithful companion, had become a victim of both me and the monstrous being I crafted. I retraced every moment of my life in my mind's eye - the peaceful joy I had once known while living with my family in Geneva, the loss of my mother,

and my departure for Ingolstadt. I trembled as I thought of my hideous adversary, and I couldn't help but recall the fateful night when he came to life. I was unable to follow this train of thought any further.

After recovering from my illness, I started taking a little bit of laudanum each night to help me sleep. It was the only way I could get the rest I needed to stay alive. But on this particular night, burdened by the memories of my many misfortunes, I took double my usual dose and quickly fell into a deep sleep. Unfortunately, sleep did not bring me any relief from my thoughts and misery. Instead, my dreams were filled with terrifying images. Towards morning, I experienced a kind of nightmarish state. I felt as though the fiend was gripping my neck, and I couldn't escape. I heard groans and cries all around me. My father, who was keeping watch, noticed my restlessness and woke me up. I realized I was surrounded by crashing waves and a cloudy sky. The fiend was nowhere to be seen. A sense of safety washed over me, as if there was a temporary truce between the present moment and the inevitable, disastrous future. This feeling brought me a temporary peace, a momentary forgetfulness that the human mind is uniquely capable of.

CHAPTER

TWENTY-TWO

291 OUR JOURNEY CAME TO AN END, and we arrived in Paris. It became clear to me that I had pushed myself too hard and needed rest before continuing. My father took great care of me, but he didn't understand the true cause of my suffering and tried ineffective methods to cure my incurable illness. He wanted me to socialize and find amusement in society, but I couldn't stand being around people. No, it's not that I couldn't stand them! They were my fellow humans, my brethren, and I felt drawn to even the most repulsive among them, seeing them as angelic beings. However, I believed I had no right to be in their company. I had unleashed an enemy among them, someone who delighted in causing them harm and reveling in their pain. If they knew about my unholy actions and the crimes I had committed, they would all despise me and drive me away from the world!

Eventually, my father gave in to my desire to avoid society and tried to convince me that there was hope, using different arguments. At times, he thought that my despair stemmed from feeling ashamed of being accused of murder, and he tried to show me that pride was pointless.

292 "Oh no, Father," I sighed, "you don't understand me at all. It would be degrading for humanity if someone as monstrous as I am were to feel any sense of pride. Justine, poor Justine, she was as innocent as me, yet she suffered the same accusation and paid with her life. And it was all because of me—I murdered her. William, Justine, Henry... they all died because of me."

During my time in captivity, I had often confessed this very same guilt to my father. Sometimes he seemed to want an explanation, while other times he dismissed it as the product of my delirium. He believed that during my illness, I had conjured up this idea in my feverish imagination and clung to it during my recovery. I avoided going into further detail and maintained an unwavering silence about the creature I had created. I was convinced that if I were to speak openly, I would be labeled mad, and that alone was enough to keep my lips sealed. But, beyond that, I couldn't bring myself to reveal a secret that would fill my father with terror and unnatural horror. So, I suppressed my desperate need for understanding and kept quiet when all I wanted was to confide in someone about this terrible secret. Yet, despite my efforts, words like the ones I just shared would sometimes burst out uncontrollably. I couldn't explain them, but speaking them out loud brought a minor relief to the weight of my mysterious anguish.

293 On this occasion, my father was filled with astonishment and said to me, "My dear Victor, what foolishness is this? I implore you, my beloved son, never utter such a statement again."

"I am not insane," I declared passionately. "The sun and the heavens, who have witnessed my actions, can vouch for my honesty. I am responsible for the deaths of those innocent victims. They perished due to my actions."

After hearing my words, my father concluded that my thoughts were crazy. He immediately changed the subject of our conversation. He wanted to erase the memory of the events that occurred in Ireland and never mentioned them, nor allowed me to speak of my misfortunes.

As time passed, I grew more composed. Misery still resided in my heart, but I silenced the desperate voice that wished to proclaim itself to the world. My demeanor became calmer and more composed than it had been since my journey to the icy sea.

A few days before we departed Paris for Switzerland, I received a letter from Elizabeth, which read:

"My dear Friend,

I was delighted to receive a letter from my uncle in Paris. You are now closer, and I hope to see you in less than two weeks. I can only imagine how much you have suffered, my dear cousin. I expect to see you looking even worse than when you left Geneva. This winter has been miserable for me too, filled with worry. But I hope to see peace on your face and find that your heart is not completely devoid of comfort and serenity.

However, I fear that the same feelings that made you so unhappy a year ago still exist, perhaps even intensified by time. I don't want to disturb you during this difficult period, when you are burdened with so many misfortunes. But I feel compelled to provide some explanation.

You might wonder, what does Elizabeth have to explain? If you truly have this thought, then my questions are answered, and all my doubts are resolved. However, since we are separated, it's possible that you may fear and yet welcome this explanation. Considering this possibility, I can no longer delay writing what I have often wanted to express to you during your absence, but never found the courage to begin.

"You know, Victor, that our parents always wanted us to get married ever since we were little. They told us this when we were young and encouraged us to believe that it would happen for sure. We were close friends during our childhood and, I think, special and important to each other as we got older. But just like how siblings can care deeply for each other without wanting a romantic relationship, could that be the same for us? Please tell me, dear Victor. I beg

156

you, for both of our happiness, tell me honestly—do you have feelings for someone else?”

“You have traveled and spent many years at Ingolstadt. Last autumn, when I saw you so unhappy and isolating yourself from everyone, I thought that you might regret our connection and feel obligated to honor your parents' wishes, even if they go against your own desires. But that is not true. I want to confess to you, my friend, that I love you. In my dreams of the future, you have always been my constant companion and closest friend. However, I also want your happiness, not just my own. I want to tell you that our marriage would make me incredibly unhappy unless it is your own choice. Even now, I cry at the thought that your honor might prevent you from experiencing the love and happiness that could bring you back to yourself, especially when you are burdened by such immense misfortunes. As someone who truly cares for you, I might only make your miseries worse by standing in the way of your wishes. Victor, please understand that your cousin and childhood friend loves you deeply and would be miserable if you thought otherwise. Be happy, my friend. And if you grant me this one request, know that nothing in the world will be able to disturb my peace of mind.”

Please do not let this letter bother you; you don't have to reply tomorrow, or the day after, or even until we see each other, if it will make you sad. My uncle will update me about your health, and if I see just one smile on your face when we meet, because of this or anything else I've done, I won't need anything else to be happy.

Elizabeth Lavenza.

Geneva, May 18th, 17—.

THIS LETTER REMINDED me of something I had forgotten, the threat of the monster—“I will be with you on your wedding night!” That was my punishment, and on that night, the monster would do whatever it took to destroy me and take away my glimpse of happiness that had given me some comfort among my sufferings. On that night, he had made up his mind to complete his crimes by killing me. Well, let it be so; if a deadly battle was to happen, if he won, I would finally have peace and he would no longer have power over me. If I won, I would be a free man. But oh, what kind of freedom? The kind a peasant has when his family has been murdered before his eyes, his home burned down, his land destroyed, and he's left with nothing, no home, no money, and no one, but he is free. That would be my freedom, except that I still had Elizabeth, who was a treasure to me. Sadly, that treasure was weighed down by the horrors of guilt and remorse that would follow me until the end of my life.

298   Dearest Elizabeth, I carefully read and reread your letter. It stirred something within me, softening my heart and filling it with dreams of love and happiness. But I knew deep down that my fate had already been sealed, and any hope of paradise was slipping away. Still, I would give my life to bring her joy and make her happy. If the monster carried out his threat, death would be inevitable. Yet, I considered whether getting married would bring about my demise sooner. If my torturer suspected that I delayed the wedding out of fear, he would surely find other, even more horrifying ways to seek revenge. He had promised to be with me on the night of my wedding, but he did not see that as a reason to wait for his attack. To further prove this, he had already taken the life of my friend Clerval right after making his threats. Therefore, I made up my mind that if marrying my cousin immediately would bring happiness to her or my father, my enemy's plans to end my life would not stop it from happening, not even for a single hour.

299   I was in a troubled state of mind when I wrote to Elizabeth. My letter was calm and filled with love. "My beloved girl," I said, "there may not be much happiness left for us in this world, but everything that brings me joy is centered around you. Don't let your fears consume you; I dedicate my life to you and my pursuit of contentment. I have a terrible secret, Elizabeth, one that, once revealed, will horrify you and make you wonder how I have survived. I will share

this tale of misery and terror with you the day after we get married, because, my dear cousin, there must be complete trust between us. But until then, I beg you, please don't mention it or make references to it. I ask this of you sincerely, and I believe you will comply."

About a week after receiving Elizabeth's letter, we returned to Geneva. The kind-hearted girl greeted me with warm affection, although tears welled up in her eyes as she saw my frail body and feverish cheeks. I noticed a change in her as well. She had become thinner and had lost some of the radiant energy that had captivated me before. However, her gentleness and compassionate gaze made her a more suitable companion for someone as devastated and miserable as I was.

About a week after receiving Elizabeth's letter, we returned to Geneva. The kind girl greeted me with warmth, though tears filled her eyes as she saw how thin and feverish I appeared. I noticed a change in her as well. She had become thinner and had lost some of the lively spirit that had charmed me before. However, her gentleness and compassionate looks made her a better companion for someone like me, someone who was ruined and miserable.

The peace I was experiencing at that time did not last long. Memories brought madness with them, and I was consumed by real insanity when I thought about what had happened. I would sometimes become furious and filled with rage, while other times I would become low-spirited and despondent. I didn't speak or look at anyone; I simply sat there, motionless, overwhelmed by the multitude of miseries that engulfed me.

Only Elizabeth had the power to pull me out of these fits. Her gentle voice would calm me down when I was consumed by anger and awaken human emotions in me when I was submerged in apathy. She cried with me and for me. When I regained my reason, she would advise me and try to instill a sense of acceptance in me. Ah! It is good for the unfortunate to be resigned, but for the guilty, there is no peace. The torments of remorse poison the limited pleasure that can sometimes be found in indulging in excessive grief.

Shortly after my return, my father brought up the subject of my immediate marriage to Elizabeth. I remained silent.

"Do you have some other attachment?" he asked.

"None on this earth. I love Elizabeth and eagerly anticipate our union. Let the date be set, and on that day, I will dedicate myself, in life or death, to my cousin's happiness."

301 "My dear Victor, please don't speak like that. We've experienced great misfortunes, but let us hold on to what we still have and transfer our love for those we've lost to those who are still alive. Our circle may be small, but we'll be bound together by love and our shared hardships. And as time passes and your despair eases, new and precious things will come into our lives to fill the void left by those we've tragically lost."

These were the lessons my father taught me. However, I couldn't forget the threat. It's understandable that I would see the fiend as invincible, given the destruction he had caused. When he said, "I will be with you on your wedding night," I couldn't help but think that this fate was unavoidable. But if it meant losing Elizabeth, death held no fear for me. With a calm and even happy expression, I agreed with my father that if my cousin agreed, the wedding would take place in ten days, and I believed this would seal my destiny.

302 Oh, how terrible! If only I had realized the wicked intentions of my fiendish adversary, I would have rather exiled myself than agree to this marriage. But, it seemed as though the monster had a power to blind me to his true plans. I unknowingly hastened the demise of someone far dearer to me.

As the date of our wedding approached, whether out of fear or a sense of foreboding, my heart began to sink. However, I hid my emotions behind a cheerful facade, which brought smiles and happiness to my father's face, but could hardly deceive Elizabeth's observant eyes. She looked forward to our union with a calm sense of contentment, though mingled with a bit of fear, which previous misfortunes had instilled in her. She worried that what appeared to be definite and joyful happiness might soon fade away like a fragile dream, leaving behind only deep and everlasting regret.

As the day of our wedding approached, there was an air of celebration and joy surrounding us. People came to congratulate us and everyone seemed to be smiling. Deep down, however, I couldn't shake the anxiety that consumed me. I kept my worries hidden in my heart, pretending to be fully engaged in my father's plans, even though they seemed more like decorations for the tragedy that awaited me. Thankfully, my father had managed to reclaim a small part of Elizabeth's inheritance from the Austrian government. She owned a piece of land on the shores of Como, and it was decided that we would go there after our wedding to enjoy our first days as a married couple.

In the meantime, I took every precaution to protect myself in case the monster decided to attack me openly. I carried pistols and a dagger, which brought me a sense of peace and tranquility. In fact, as the wedding day approached, the threat seemed more like an illusion.

Elizabeth seemed happy, but she eventually fell into such a state of melancholy. I think she was worried about what I might eventually reveal to her. My father was in the mean time overjoyed, and, in the bustle of preparation, only recognised in the melancholy of his niece the diffidence of a bride.

After the ceremony was performed, a large party assembled at my father's, but it was agreed that Elizabeth and I should commence our journey by water, sleeping that night at Evian, and continuing our voyage on the following day.

Those were the last moments of my life during which I enjoyed the feeling of happiness. While we enjoyed the beauty of the scene from our boat, we saw Mont Salêve, the pleasant banks of Montalègre, and at a distance, surmounting all, the beautiful Mont Blanc, and the assemblage of snowy mountains that in vain endeavour to emulate her. We also saw the mighty Jura opposing its dark side to the ambition that would quit its native country, and an almost insurmountable barrier to the invader who should wish to enslave it.

305   I held Elizabeth's hand tightly. "You seem sad, my love. If only you knew the suffering I have endured and may still face. Today, at least, I am allowed a moment of calm and freedom from despair."

"Don't worry, my dear Victor," Elizabeth replied. "There is nothing to distress you. Even if my face doesn't show great joy, my heart is content. Something tells me not to put too much hope in our future, but I refuse to listen to that negative voice. Look how quickly we are moving and how the clouds above Mont Blanc make this beautiful scene even more captivating. See all the fish swimming in the crystal-clear water. We can even see every pebble at the bottom. What a perfect day! Nature looks so happy and peaceful."

Elizabeth tried to shift our focus away from sadness. However, her mood was inconsistent. Happiness briefly appeared in her eyes, only to be replaced by distraction and daydreaming.

306   As the sun began to set, we continued our journey and crossed the river Drance, marveling at how it wound its way through the deep valleys of the tall hills. The Alps drew nearer to the lake at this point, and we approached the beautiful ring of mountains that bordered its eastern side. In the midst of the surrounding woods, the church spire of Evian stood out, overshadowed by the towering range of mountains.

The previously strong wind that had been carrying us swiftly started to die down to a gentle breeze as the sun set. The soft air lightly brushed the water's surface, causing a pleasant swaying among the trees as we neared the shore. From there, we were greeted by the delightful fragrance of flowers and freshly cut hay, carried by the breeze. The sun disappeared below the horizon just as we reached the land. As my feet touched the shoreline, I felt the weight of my worries and fears return, knowing they would soon consume me and remain with me forever.

TWENTY-THREE

 It was 8 o'clock when we arrived. We walked for a little while by the shore, admiring the fading light, then went to the inn and gazed upon the beautiful view of the waters, trees, and mountains, now hidden in darkness but still visible as dark shapes.

The wind, which had died down from the south, now picked up with force from the west. The moon had reached its highest point in the sky and was beginning to descend. The clouds moved swiftly across it, faster than a vulture in flight, reducing its brightness. Meanwhile, the lake reflected the busy scene of the sky, made even busier by the restless waves that were starting to form. Suddenly, a heavy storm of rain poured down.

I had been calm earlier in the day, but as soon as nightfall concealed the shapes of objects, a thousand fears flooded my mind. I became anxious and watchful, my right hand clutching a concealed pistol in my bosom. Every sound scared me, but I was determined to defend myself, not hesitating until either my adversary's life or my own life was extinguished.

Elizabeth noticed my agitation, remaining silent for some time out of timidity and fear. However, something in my expression filled her with terror, causing her to tremble as she asked, "What is troubling you, my dear Victor? What is it that you fear?"

"Please, my love, be at peace," I replied. "Tonight, everything will be safe. But I must admit, tonight is extremely dreadful."

308   I spent an hour in this anxious state of mind, when it dawned on me how terrifying the expected confrontation would be for my wife. I begged her to go to a safe place, promising to join her once I had gathered information about the whereabouts of my enemy.

She left me, and I paced the hallways of the house for some time, carefully checking every corner where my adversary could hide. However, I found no sign of him, and began to wonder if some stroke of luck had prevented him from carrying out his threats. Then, suddenly, I heard a piercing and terrifying scream. It came from the room where Elizabeth had gone. Every muscle in my body froze, and I could feel the rush of blood through my veins, a tingling sensation in my limbs. This state lasted only for a moment before the scream sounded again, and without hesitation, I rushed into the room.

309   Goodness gracious! Why didn't I just die right then and there! Why am I still alive to tell the tale of the destruction of the best of hopes and the purest being on this earth? There she was, lifeless and motionless, lying across the bed with her head hanging down, her pale and distorted face partially covered by her hair. Everywhere I look, I see the same sight—her ghostly arms and limp body thrown by the killer onto its funeral bed. How could I witness this and still carry on? Oh, life is stubborn, clinging tightly even where it is most despised. For only a moment, I lost consciousness; I fell to the ground, completely unaware.

When I came to, I found myself surrounded by the people from the inn. Their faces showed sheer terror, but their horror seemed insignificant compared to the overwhelming feelings that consumed me. I escaped from them and made my way to the room where lay Elizabeth's lifeless body. She was my love, my wife, so recently alive, so dear, so deserving. They had changed her position from when I first saw her; now she lay with her head on her arm, a handkerchief placed across her face and neck. I could have mistaken her for being asleep. I rushed towards her, embracing her with all my might, but the lifelessness and coldness of her limbs told me that the Elizabeth I now held in my arms was no longer the one I had loved and adored. The devil's murderous grip had left its mark on her neck, and her breath had ceased to escape from her lips.

As I grieved over her with intense sadness, I happened to glance up. The room, once dimly lit, became illuminated by the pale yellow glow of the moon, causing a wave of fear to wash over me. The shutters had been thrown open, and with utter horror, I saw a figure, grotesque and repulsive, standing at the window. A wicked grin adorned the monster's face as he cruelly pointed his finger towards my wife's lifeless body. Without hesitation, I lunged towards the window, quickly retrieving a pistol from my pocket, and fired a shot. However, he evaded me, leaping from his perch and, with lightning speed, plunging into the nearby lake.

The sound of the gunshot attracted a crowd into the room. I gestured towards the spot where the creature had vanished, and we embarked on boats, searching the waters with nets. Our efforts were in vain. After spending countless hours, we returned, dejected and hopeless. Many of my companions believed that it was a figment of my imagination. After disembarking, they fanned out, scouring the surrounding countryside, dividing into groups and exploring the woods and vineyards in every direction.

I tried to go with them, and walked a short distance from the house. But I felt dizzy and stumbled like a drunk person. Eventually, I collapsed from exhaustion. My vision blurred, and my skin was hot and dry from fever. They brought me back and laid me on a bed. I was barely aware of what had happened, but my eyes scanned the room, searching for something lost.

After a while, I got up and instinctively crawled into the room where my beloved's body lay. There were women crying around me. I leaned over the body and wept with them. During that time, my mind was a jumble of thoughts. I couldn't grasp a clear idea, but my mind wandered between various subjects, reflecting on my misfortunes and their cause. I was lost in a fog of astonishment and horror. William's death, the wrongful execution of Justine, the murder of Clerval, and finally, the death of my wife. At that moment, I didn't even know if my only remaining loved ones were safe from the fiend's malevolence. My father might be suffering in his clutches, and Ernest could be dead at his feet. The thought sent shivers down my spine and snapped me back into action. I stood up and made up my mind to return to Geneva as quickly as possible.

312   There were no horses available, so I had to return by the lake. Unfortunately, the wind was not in my favor, and the rain was pouring down heavily. Despite the unfavorable conditions, it was still early in the morning, and I had hope that I could make it back by nightfall. I hired men to row the boat, and I took an oar myself. I had always found solace from mental pain through physical activity. However, the overwhelming anguish I was feeling and the extreme agitation I was experiencing made it impossible for me to exert any effort. I threw down the oar and rested my head in my hands, surrendering to every gloomy thought that crossed my mind. Whenever I looked up, I saw the familiar scenery that had once brought me joy, the same scenes I had admired with the one who now exists only as a memory and a shadow. Tears streamed down my face. For a brief moment, the rain subsided, and I saw the fish swimming in the water, just as they had been observed by Elizabeth a few hours before. There is nothing more painful to the human mind than a sudden and dramatic change. The sun might still shine, or the clouds might darken the sky, but nothing appeared to me how it did the day before. A demon had snatched away all hope of future happiness from me. I don't think anyone has ever been as miserable as I am right now. Such a horrifying event is unparalleled in the history of humanity.

313   But why should I go into detail about what happened next? My story has been filled with horrifying events, reaching a climax, and what I have left to tell may seem boring to you. Just know that, one

by one, my friends were taken from me, leaving me all alone. I am worn out, and I'll try to sum up the rest of my terrible story in a few words.

I arrived in Geneva. My father and Ernest were still alive, but my father couldn't bear the news I brought. I can still see him in my mind, a great and respected old man. His eyes had lost their sparkle, for they had lost the joy they once held. His love for Elizabeth, who he treated as more than a daughter, was deep and profound. It was the kind of love that a person feels when they are older and have few remaining attachments, so they hold on tightly to the ones they have. I curse the monster that brought misery to my father's gray hair and sentenced him to suffer in despair. The horrors that surrounded him were too much to bear, and suddenly, the will to live left him. He couldn't even get out of bed, and a few days later, he died in my arms.

What happened to me then? I don't know. I lost consciousness, and all I could feel were the weight of chains and the darkness surrounding me. Sometimes, I would dream that I was wandering in beautiful meadows and pleasant valleys with my friends from long ago, but then I would wake up and find myself in a prison cell. Sadness followed, but gradually I began to understand the extent of my sorrows and my situation, and that's when they released me from my confinement. You see, my mental health was monitored for many months, and i was kept in seclusion.

However, freedom meant nothing to me if I did not also awaken to reason and a desire for revenge. As the memories of past tragedies overwhelmed me, I started to contemplate their cause—the monster that I had brought to life, the wretched creature that I had unleashed upon the world to destroy me. Anger consumed me whenever I thought of him, and I yearned to have him in my clutches so I could get revenge.

And my hatred did not remain mere wishful thinking for long; I began to ponder the best ways to capture him. For this purpose, about a month after my release, I sought out a criminal judge in town, telling him that I had an accusation to make. I claimed to know the murderer who had destroyed my family and demanded that he use his full authority to apprehend this killer.

315 The judge listened to me with attention and kindness, assuring me that he would spare no efforts to catch the criminal.

"Thank you," I replied. "Please listen to my statement. It's a bizarre tale, and I fear you may not believe it if it weren't for the undeniable truth within. The story is too coherent to be mistaken for a dream, and I have no reason to lie." I spoke to him calmly yet impressively, as I had made a firm resolution in my heart to pursue my destroyer until they paid for their actions. This purpose calmed my pain and, for a while, made me accept my life. I told him my history, briefly but accurately, emphasizing the important dates and avoiding any anger or exclamations.

At first, the judge seemed incredulous, but as I continued, he grew more attentive and interested. I could see horror on his face at times, and at other times, a mixture of surprise and belief.

When I finished my story, I declared, "This is the person I accuse, and I demand that you use all your power to catch and punish them. It is your duty as a judge, and I trust that as a human being, you will not shy away from fulfilling that duty."

316 The words I spoke seemed to have a profound effect on the magistrate. At first, he listened to my story with a skeptical curiosity, as if it were just another tale of ghosts and supernatural occurrences. But now that I was seeking his official assistance, his doubts resurfaced. He responded in a calm tone, "I am willing to help you in your pursuit, but the creature you describe possesses powers that would make it difficult for me to act. How can one chase after a being that can traverse icy seas and dwell in caves and dens where no one would dare to go? Additionally, it has been several months since these crimes occurred, and no one can speculate on where he has gone or where he may be now."

"I am convinced that he is lurking somewhere close to where I reside. If he has sought refuge in the Alps, we can track him down like we do with chamois and eliminate him as a predator. However, I can sense your doubts. You do not believe my account and do not plan to pursue my enemy and give him the punishment he deserves."

As I spoke, anger burned in my eyes, causing the magistrate to feel intimidated. "You are mistaken," he said, attempting to regain his composure. "I will do everything in my power to capture this monster and ensure he faces appropriate punishment for his crimes. However, based on the qualities you've described, it may prove to be impossible. While we take all the necessary steps, you must prepare yourself for the possibility of disappointment."

"That cannot be accepted. But I understand that my desire for revenge is insignificant to you. Yet, I must confess that it consumes my soul, becoming the sole passion within me. I am overwhelmed with rage when I consider that the murderer, whom I have unleashed upon society, still exists. You deny my justified plea, leaving me with only one option: to dedicate myself to his destruction, regardless of whether it costs me my life."

As I said this, I trembled with intense agitation. My mannerisms exhibited a certain frenzy, and perhaps even a trace of the haughty fierceness attributed to the martyrs of old. However, to a magistrate from Geneva, whose mind was preoccupied with matters far different from devotion and heroism, my elevated state of mind likely appeared as madness. He tried to calm me down, approaching me with the tenderness of a nurse soothing a child, and dismissed my story as the product of delirium.

"Man," I cried out, overwhelmed by his lack of understanding, "how uninformed you are in your ignorant pride of wisdom! Cease speaking, for you do not comprehend the weight of your words."

I stormed away from the house full of anger and upset, and went off by myself to think about a different plan of what to do.

CHAPTER
TWENTY-FOUR

319   I WAS in a situation where I couldn't think clearly. I was consumed by anger and revenge, which gave me strength and control over my emotions. It allowed me to stay calm and collected, even when I should have been going crazy or giving up.

My first decision was to leave Geneva forever. My home country, which used to be dear to me when I was happy and loved, now became a place of hatred. I gathered some money and a few pieces of jewelry that had belonged to my mother, and left.

And so, my journey began, one that will only end when I die. I have traveled through many parts of the world, enduring the hardships that explorers in deserts and uncivilized lands face. I don't even know how I managed to survive; there were many times when I collapsed on the sandy ground, wishing for death. But my desire for revenge kept me alive. I couldn't die and let my enemy continue to live.

320   When I left Geneva, my first task was to find some clue that could help me track down my merciless enemy. But my plan was uncertain, and I spent many hours wandering near the edges of the town, unsure of which direction to take. As evening approached, I found

myself standing at the entrance of the graveyard where William, Elizabeth, and my father were laid to rest. I went inside and approached the tomb that marked their graves. Everything was quiet, except for the rustling of the leaves in the trees, gently moved by the wind. The night was almost completely dark, and the scene would have been solemn and moving even to someone who wasn't directly involved. It felt as though the spirits of the departed were floating nearby, casting a presence that could be sensed but not seen, surrounding the grieving mourner.

As I left Geneva, my first task was to find some clue that would help me track down the person who had done this evil to me. But I didn't have a clear plan, so I wandered around outside the town for many hours, not sure which direction to go. As it got dark, I found myself at the entrance of the graveyard where William, Elizabeth, and my father were buried. I went inside and approached their tomb. It was silent, except for the sound of leaves rustling in the wind. The night was almost completely dark, and the scene would have been solemn and moving even to someone who wasn't affected. It felt like the spirits of the departed were hovering around, casting a shadow over me, the mourner.

The intense grief I felt at first quickly turned into anger and hopelessness. They were dead, and I was alive. The person who killed them was also alive, and I had to live with that fact. I kneeled on the grass and kissed the ground. With trembling lips, I said, "I swear by the ground I'm kneeling on, by the spirits that are near me, and by the deep and eternal grief I feel, I promise to pursue the monster responsible for this misery until either he or I perish in a final battle. For this purpose, I will stay alive. I will see the sun again and walk on the green earth, which would otherwise disappear from my sight forever. I call on you, spirits of the dead, and you, avengers who wander, to help and guide me in my quest. Make the cursed and evil creature suffer greatly; let him feel the same despair that torments me."

I started my oath with seriousness and a feeling that the spirits of my murdered friends were listening and supporting me, but as I finished, anger took over and I couldn't speak anymore.

322   In the stillness of the night, a loud and evil laugh broke the silence. It echoed through the mountains. The laughter eventually faded, but then a familiar and loathed voice whispered audibly near my ear, "I am content. You wretched creature, you've chosen to live, and I am content."

In an instant, I lunged towards the source of the sound, but the devil slipped away from my grasp. Just then, the full moon emerged, casting its light upon his horrifying and distorted form as he fled with supernatural swiftness.

I pursued him relentlessly, dedicating many months to this task. Following a faint clue, I tracked the winding path of the Rhone River, but to no avail. Eventually, the vast expanse of the Mediterranean Sea came into view, and by some fortuitous turn of events, I witnessed the fiend sneaking aboard a ship heading for the Black Sea under the cover of night. I secured a spot on the same vessel, but somehow he managed to elude me once again, and I remain uncertain as to how.

323   In the wilderness of Tartary and Russia, despite his elusiveness, I have always followed his trail. Sometimes frightened villagers would inform me of his whereabouts, fearing this horrifying apparition. Other times, he himself, perhaps fearing that if I lost all trace of him, I would lose hope and die, left some sign for me to follow. As the snow fell upon my head, I saw the imprint of his large footstep on the vast white plain. How can you, who are just beginning your journey through life, fathom the depths of what I have felt, and still feel? Cold, hunger, and exhaustion were the least of my sufferings; I was cursed by some evil force, carrying my eternal torment with me. Yet, amid it all, a spirit of goodness guided and directed my steps. Just when I thought I could bear no more, it would rescue me from seemingly insurmountable obstacles. Sometimes, when nature was overcome by hunger and I could go no further, a meal would miraculously appear in the wilderness, restoring and invigorating me. It

was a simple fare, like that eaten by the local villagers, but I cannot doubt that it was placed there by the spirits I had called upon for assistance. And often, when everything was dry, the sky cloudless, and my thirst consuming me, a brief cloud would appear, bringing the few drops of water that revived me before vanishing.

I tried to stay near the rivers whenever possible, but the creature I pursued usually avoided those areas. In other places, it was rare to encounter other human beings, and I mainly survived by hunting the wild animals I came across.

My life was terrible, but sleep brought me joy. Oh, how I cherished sleep! Even in my worst moments, it gave me moments of ecstasy. The spirits that protected me granted me these moments of happiness, so that I could find the strength to continue my journey. Without this rest, I would have been overwhelmed by the difficulties I faced. During the day, I was sustained by the hope of sleep. In my dreams, I saw my loved ones, my wife, and my beloved homeland. I saw my father's kind face, heard my dear Elizabeth's voice, and watched Clerval enjoying health and youth. Often, when I was exhausted from a long journey, I convinced myself that I was dreaming and that night would bring reality and the embrace of my dearest friends. How intense was my love for them! I clung to their memory, even during my waking hours, convincing myself that they were still alive. In those moments, the burning desire for vengeance in my heart would fade away, and I pursued my mission to destroy the monster more out of a sense of duty imposed by a higher power, an instinctive force that I was not fully aware of, rather than as a fervent desire of my soul.

I cannot know what the man I was chasing felt. Sometimes he left messages on trees or stones that guided me and fueled my anger. "My power is not yet gone," (these words were written in one of the inscriptions); "you are alive, and I have complete control. Follow me, I am heading to the freezing north, where you will experience the misery of cold and frost, which do not affect me. If you don't follow too slowly, you will find a dead hare nearby; eat it to replenish yourself. Come, my enemy; we still have to fight for our lives, but you will endure many difficult and miserable hours before that time comes."

You wicked devil! I vow revenge once again; I dedicate you, pitiful monster, to torment and death. I will never stop searching until either he or I die; and then, with what joy shall I reunite with my beloved Elizabeth and my departed friends, who even now prepare for me the reward of my long and dreadful journey!

As I continued my journey towards the north, the snow thickened, and the cold became almost unbearable. The villagers stayed in their huts, and only a few brave ones ventured out to catch the animals that had come out of hiding in search of food. The rivers were frozen, and there were no fish to be found; thus, I was cut off from my main source of food.

The triumph of my enemy grew stronger as my labors became more difficult. One message he left said: "Get ready! Your struggles are just beginning. Bundle up in warm fur and gather provisions, for we are about to embark on a journey where your suffering will satisfy my eternal hatred."

These mocking words only fueled my courage and determination. I swore to myself that I would not give up on my mission. With unwavering fervor, I continued to trek through vast deserts, praying to God for strength. Finally, in the distance, I saw the ocean, marking the farthest edge of the horizon. But it was nothing like the serene blue waters of the south. Instead, it was covered in ice, rough and untamed. The ancient Greeks wept tears of joy when they caught sight of the Mediterranean from the hills of Asia, celebrating the end of their arduous journey. I did not weep, but I knelt down and thanked my guiding spirit with a grateful heart for leading me safely to this place. Despite my adversary's taunts, I hoped to confront and confront him here.

A few weeks before this time, I had obtained a sled and dogs so that I could travel quickly through the snowy terrain. I'm not sure if my enemy had the same means of transportation, but I noticed that while I had been falling behind in my pursuit before, now I was closing in on him. By the time I caught sight of the ocean, he was only one day ahead of me, and I hoped to catch up to him before he reached the beach. Filled with renewed determination, I continued onward and arrived at a small, miserable village near the coast after two days. I asked the villagers about the fiend and gathered reliable information. They told me that a colossal monster had arrived the previous night, armed with a gun and several pistols. The terrifying sight of him had caused the scared inhabitants of a solitary cottage to flee. He had taken their winter food supply and loaded it onto a sled, which he then attached to a large group of trained dogs. To the horror of the villagers, that same night, he embarked on a journey across the sea in a direction that did not lead to any land. They speculated that he would likely be destroyed by the breaking ice or frozen in the eternal cold very soon.

329 Upon hearing this information, a wave of despair washed over me. The fiend had eluded me, and now I had to embark on a treacherous and seemingly endless journey across the icy mountains of the ocean. The cold in those regions was unbearable, even for the toughest individuals, and as a person from a warm and sunny climate, I knew I couldn't hope to survive. However, despite the overwhelming odds, my fierce anger and desire for revenge against the fiend resurfaced. I prepared for my journey.

I exchanged my regular sledge for one specifically designed for the uneven surfaces of the Frozen Ocean. I also stocked up on ample provisions.

I cannot say for certain how many days have passed since then, but I have endured extreme suffering in the hopes of exacting revenge. Immense and jagged ice mountains often blocked my path, and I frequently heard the ominous rumblings of the sea beneath, threatening to consume me. Yet, I continued on my way.

330 Based on the amount of food I had consumed, I estimate that I had been on this journey for about three weeks. The constant prolongation of hope, only to have it fade away again, often made me feel deeply despondent and filled my eyes with bitter tears of

sadness. Despair was close to claiming me completely, and I was on the verge of being overwhelmed by this hardship. Once, after the exhausted animals carrying me had made an extraordinarily difficult climb to the top of a sloping ice-covered mountain, one of them, unable to bear the fatigue any longer, died. Looking out over the vast plain ahead, I felt a great anguish. However, in that very moment, my eyes caught sight of a small dark shape in the distance. Straining my sight to get a better view, my heart filled with ecstasy as I realized it was a sled and the distorted figure within it was someone I knew well. Oh, how an intense feeling of hope rushed back into my heart! Warm tears filled my eyes, but I quickly wiped them away so they wouldn't obstruct my view of the monster. However, even as I wiped away the tears, my vision was still blurred, and overcome by the overwhelming emotions that gripped me, I couldn't help but cry out loud.

331   But this was not the time to wait. I removed the dead dog from the sled, gave the remaining dogs enough food, and after resting for an hour, which was necessary but frustrating, I continued on my journey. I could still see the sled. There were only a few times when it disappeared behind ice formations. I was even able to catch up to it, and after traveling for nearly two days, I could see my enemy only a mile away. I was filled with excitement.

But just when I thought I was about to catch my enemy, my hopes were crushed. I completely lost sight of him, more than ever before. I heard a rumbling under the ice, and the thunderous sound of waves growing larger and more threatening. I tried to keep moving, but it was futile. The wind picked up, the sea roared, and with a tremendous and terrifying noise, the ice split and cracked like an earthquake. It all happened so quickly. In a matter of minutes, a chaotic sea separated me from my enemy. I was left drifting on a shrinking piece of ice, facing a gruesome death.

332   In this way, many terrifying hours went by. Some of my dogs died, and I was on the verge of collapsing from the overwhelming distress. That's when I spotted your ship anchored nearby, offering

me hope of help and survival. I never imagined that ships would venture this far north, so I was amazed by the sight. I quickly dismantled part of my sled to fashion makeshift oars. With tremendous effort, I managed to steer my ice raft towards your ship. Even if you had been heading south, I had made up my mind to rely on the sea's mercy rather than abandon my mission. I had hoped to convince you to lend me a boat so that I could continue my pursuit of my enemy. However, your course was northward. You rescued me when I was completely worn out, and I would have soon perished from the numerous hardships I endured—a fate I still fear because my mission remains unfinished.

Oh! When will my guiding spirit lead me to the monster, so I can finally find rest? Or must I die while he still lives? If I do, promise me, Walton, that he will not escape. Promise me that you will seek him out and satisfy my desire for vengeance by killing him. And yet, do I dare to ask you to undertake the hardships that I have endured? No, I am not that selfish. But when I am dead, if he should appear to you, if the agents of vengeance bring him to you, promise me that he will not live. Promise me that he will not triumph over my countless sufferings and continue to commit his dark crimes. He is skilled in speaking and convincing, and his words once had power over my heart. But do not trust him. His soul is as evil as his appearance, filled with deceit and cruel malice. Do not listen to him. Instead, call upon the spirits of William, Justine, Clerval, Elizabeth, my father, and the miserable Victor, and thrust your sword into his heart. I will stay close by, guiding your hand so that the blade strikes true.

WALTON, continuing his narrative.

August 26th, 17—.

You have read this strange and scary story, Margaret. Do you not feel your blood chill with fear, like mine does right now? Sometimes, overcome with sudden pain, he couldn't continue his tale. Other times, his voice, though shaky, managed to utter the words filled with anguish. His beautiful eyes were now filled with anger, now filled with sorrow, and drowned in endless misery. Sometimes he controlled his face and voice, narrating the most horrific incidents with a calm tone, suppressing any sign of distress. Then, like a volcano erupting, his face would suddenly turn to a look of wild rage as he shouted curses at his tormentor.

His story is logical and told with the appearance of honesty, yet I confess to you that the letters from Felix and Safie he showed me, and the sight of the monster from our ship, convinced me more than his earnest affirmations. So, such a monster really exists! I cannot doubt it; yet I am astonished and amazed. Sometimes I tried to get Frankenstein to share the details of his creation: but he was unwilling to disclose that information.

335   "Are you crazy, my friend?" he asked. "Or where is your senseless curiosity leading you? Do you want to create a demonic enemy for yourself and the world? Calm down, calm down! Listen to my sorrows and don't try to add to your own."

Frankenstein noticed that I was taking notes about his story. He asked to see them and then made corrections and additions in many places, especially when adding life and emotion to the conversations he had with his enemy. "Since you have preserved my account," he said, "I don't want an incomplete version to be passed down to future generations."

336   A whole week has passed, during which I have been captivated by the most extraordinary story ever imagined. This tale, along with the refined and kind manner of my guest, has consumed my thoughts and emotions. I want to comfort him, yet is it wise to advise someone so inconsolably miserable and devoid of any hope to continue living? No, it is not. The only comfort he can find now is in finding peace and release from his torment. However, there is one comfort he enjoys, born out of solitude and madness: he believes that when he dreams of conversing with his friends, they are not mere figments of his imagination, but actual beings from a distant

realm. This belief gives his reveries a solemnity that is almost as compelling as the truth itself.

Our discussions are not always focused on his personal history and misfortunes. He possesses extensive knowledge in various fields of literature and has a keen understanding. His eloquence is powerful and moving, and I cannot help but shed tears when he recounts a heartbreaking event or attempts to stir feelings of compassion or love. In his days of prosperity, he must have been a remarkable being, now truly noble and godlike even in his downfall. He seems to recognize his own worth and the magnitude of his tragic fall.

"When I was younger," he said, "I thought I was meant for something great. I had deep feelings, but I also had a level-headedness that made me suitable for impressive accomplishments. This belief in my own worth kept me going when others would have been overwhelmed, because I saw it as a waste to indulge in pointless sorrow when I possessed talents that could benefit others. When I considered the work I had completed, which was nothing less than creating a sensitive and rational being, I couldn't lump myself together with ordinary dreamers. But now, this thought that once fueled me at the beginning of my journey only brings me further down into despair. All my ideas and hopes now mean nothing, and I feel trapped in a never-ending hell, like the archangel who aspired for omnipotence. My imagination used to be vivid, and my ability to analyze and apply myself was intense. It was with these qualities that I conceived and brought to life a human being. Even now, I cannot recall my daydreams while the work was still incomplete without feeling intense emotions. I soared among the heavens in my mind, sometimes reveling in my powers, sometimes burning with thoughts of their consequences. From a young age, I was filled with great hopes and lofty ambitions, but look at me now! Oh, my friend, if you had known me as I once was, you would not recognize me in this state of utter despair. I rarely used to feel despondent; I always believed I had a grand destiny that would carry me forward, until I fell, never, ever to rise again."

338   Do I have to lose this amazing person? I have wanted a friend for so long, someone who would understand and care about me. Look, in the middle of these empty oceans, I have found that person, but I'm afraid I have only found them to realize their worth and then lose them. I want to help them find happiness, but they are rejecting that idea.

339   "I appreciate your kindness, Walton," he said, "for wanting to help a miserable person like me. But when you mention finding new connections and forming fresh attachments, do you really believe that anyone can replace the ones I've lost? Can anyone be to me what Clerval was, or can any woman be another Elizabeth? Even when our emotions aren't deeply stirred by their exceptional qualities, child-hood companions always have a certain influence on our minds that few later friends can attain. I cherished friends who were dear to me not only out of habit and familiarity, but because of their own merits. And no matter where I am, the comforting sound of Eliza-beth's voice and the conversations I had with Clerval will always echo in my thoughts. But, they are gone. If I were engaged in an endeavor that could greatly benefit humanity, then I could continue living to fulfill it. But that is not my fate. I must pursue and eliminate the being whom I brought into existence. Only then will my purpose on earth be fulfilled, and I may finally die."

340   September 2nd.

My dear Sister,

I'm writing to you from a dangerous situation, unsure if I will ever see England or our dear friends again. I am surrounded by huge masses of ice, trapped with no way to escape, and the constant threat of our ship being crushed. The brave men who agreed to join me on this journey look to me for help, but I have nothing to offer them. Our situation is incredibly frightening, but I'm trying to stay brave and hopeful. It's terrifying to think that the lives of these men are in danger because of my foolish plans.

I can't help but wonder, Margaret, how you'll be feeling. I hope you won't hear of our potential demise and anxiously wait for my return. Years may pass, and you may have moments of despair mixed with hope. Oh, my dear sister, the thought of your heart sinking with disappointment is more agonizing to me than the possibility of my own death. But you have a loving husband and beautiful children; you can find happiness. May Heaven bless you and bring that happiness to you!

My unfortunate guest regards me with the tenderest compassion. He endeavours to fill me with hope and talks as if life were a possession which he valued. He reminds me how often the same accidents have happened to other navigators, who have attempted this sea, and, in spite of myself, he fills me with cheerful stories.

September 5th.

A scene has just passed of such uncommon interest, that although it is highly probable that these papers may never reach you, yet I cannot forbear recording it.

We are still surrounded by mountains of ice, still in danger of being crushed. The cold is excessive, and many of my unfortunate comrades have already found a grave here. Frankenstein has daily declined in health, though he sometimes shows glimmers of life.

In my previous letter, I mentioned my concerns about a potential mutiny. Today, while observing the weary expression on my friend's face, his eyes half closed and his body slumped, I was interrupted by a group of sailors who demanded to enter the cabin. They entered and their leader spoke to me. They said we were trapped in ice, with little chance of escape. They feared that if by some miracle the ice melted and a safe passage opened, I would foolishly continue our voyage and lead them into more danger, despite their hard-fought survival. They insisted that I make a promise to change our course southward if we were to be freed.

This speech troubled me. I had not given up hope, nor had I considered returning if we were liberated. However, was it fair or even possible for me to deny their demand? I hesitated before answering, but then Frankenstein, who had been silent and barely able to speak, suddenly regained his strength. His eyes gleamed and his cheeks flushed momentarily with vigor. Addressing the men, he said-

343   "What do you mean? What are you asking of me, your captain? Are you so easily giving up on your plan? Didn't you call this an amazing journey? And why was it amazing? Not because the path was smooth and calm like a tropical sea, but because it was filled with dangers and terror. You were meant to be hailed as heroes of humanity! Your names are to be praised as those of brave men who faced death for honor and the greater good. And now, look at you, at the first hint of danger, or if you prefer, the first great test of your courage, you retreat and are content to be remembered as men who lacked the strength to endure the cold and danger; and so, with pitiful souls, you became cold and returned to your comfortable firesides. That doesn't require all this preparation; you didn't need to come this far and bring your captain to the shame of defeat just to prove you were cowards. Oh, be men, or even more than men. Stay strong in your goals, as unfaltering as a mighty rock. This ice is not as unyielding as your hearts may seem; it can change, and it cannot withstand you if you decide it won't. Do not go back to your families with the shame of defeat on your faces. Return as heroes who fought and conquered, who never knew the meaning of fleeing from the enemy."

344   He said all of this with a voice that changed to match the different emotions in his words. His eyes were filled with determination and bravery. Can you understand why these men were moved by his words? They looked at each other, unable to respond. I told them to go and think about what he had said. I said that if they strongly disagreed, I wouldn't lead them further north. But I hoped that after thinking it over, their courage would return.

They left and I turned to my friend, but he was weak and almost lifeless.

I don't know how all of this will end, but I would rather die than return in shame without fulfilling my purpose. However, I fear that is what will happen. The men, without the belief in glory and honor, can't keep enduring their current hardships.

September 7th.

The decision has been made. I have agreed to return, unless something destroys us. My hopes have been crushed by cowardice and indecision. I am coming back without achieving what I wanted. It takes more patience than I have to handle this unfairness.

September 12th.

It's done. I am going back to England. I have lost my hopes for doing something useful and earning glory. I have also lost my friend. But I will try to explain all of these painful events to you, my dear sister. While I am sailing towards England and towards you, I won't lose hope.

On September 9th, something alarming happened. The ice around us started to move and make a loud, thunderous sound. It was splitting and cracking all over the place. We were in serious danger. All we could do was wait and hope for the best. Meanwhile, my unfortunate guest was getting even sicker. He was so ill that he couldn't even get out of bed. As we continued to sail, the ice was cracking and pushing us north. Then, a breeze came from the west, and on the 11th, the way south was completely clear. When the sailors saw this, they erupted in joyful shouts. They were so happy because it meant they would soon be back home in England.

When my friend, Frankenstein, woke up from his nap and heard the commotion, he asked what was going on. I explained to him that they were shouting because they were going back to England.

"Do you really plan to go back too?" he asked.

"Unfortunately, yes. I can't refuse their demand. I can't lead them into danger against their will, so I have to go back."

"You can go if you want, but I won't. My mission is given to me by a higher power, and I can't ignore it. I may be weak, but I believe the spirits helping me seek revenge will give me the strength I need."

He tried to get out of bed, but it was too much for him. He fell back and passed out.

346   It took a while before he recovered, and I was convinced that he was completely lifeless. But finally, he opened his eyes. Breathing was hard for him, and he couldn't speak. The doctor gave him a calming drink and instructed us to give him some space. Meanwhile, the doctor revealed to me that my friend only had a few hours left to live.

347   His punishment was declared, and I could only feel sorrow and wait patiently. I sat beside his bed, observing him; his eyes were shut, and I assumed he was asleep. But soon, he beckoned me in a weak voice and, asking me to come closer, he said, "Oh, how weak I have become; I know my time on this earth is limited, and yet my enemy, the one who tormented me, may still live. Don't think, Walton, that in my final moments I still harbor that burning hatred and intense desire for revenge that I once expressed. However, I do feel justified in wishing for the death of my adversary. In these last days, I have reflected on my past actions, and I find them not worthy of blame. In a state of passionate madness, I brought forth a rational being and I was obligated to ensure his happiness and well-being to the best of my abilities. That was my duty, but there was another duty even more important. My obligations towards the beings of my own kind held greater priority because they consisted of a larger amount of happiness or suffering. Motivated by this perspective, I declined, and I was correct in declining, to create a companion for the first creature. He exhibited unparalleled malevolence and self-centeredness in his wickedness: he took the lives of my friends; he condemned to destruction beings who possessed exquisite feelings, happiness, and wisdom. And I do not know where this thirst for revenge will end. In his own misery, he strives to make others equally wretched, and for that, he should meet his end. The responsibility of his demise was mine, but I have failed. When driven by selfish and immoral motives, I implored you to complete my unfin-

ished work. And now, I make this request again, driven solely by logic and virtue."

However, I cannot request that you give up your homeland and loved ones to complete this task. Furthermore, now that you are returning to England, the chances of encountering him are slim. But the weighing of these factors and the consideration of what you believe are your responsibilities are for you to decide. My judgment and thoughts are already clouded by the imminent approach of death. I cannot dare ask you to do what I believe is right, as my emotions may still misguide me.

The knowledge that he may continue to bring harm troubles me deeply. Yet, in every other aspect, this moment, when I anticipate my release, is the only joyful one I have experienced in many years. The apparitions of my beloved departed loved ones appear before me, and I eagerly anticipate joining them. Farewell, Walton! Seek happiness in calmness and shy away from ambition, even if it seems harmless, like striving for recognition in the field of science and discoveries. But why do I say this? My own hopes in these endeavors have been shattered, but perhaps someone else will succeed.

As he spoke, his voice grew weaker, and eventually, drained by his effort, he fell silent. Approximately thirty minutes later, he made another attempt to speak but was unable to. He weakly squeezed my hand, and his eyes closed forever, while the glow of a gentle smile faded from his lips.

Margaret, I am at a loss for words to describe the sadness I feel for the untimely loss of this remarkable person. No matter what I say, it will not capture the depth of my sorrow. I am overcome with tears, and my mind is clouded with disappointment. However, as I travel back to England, I hope to find some comfort there.

I apologize for the interruption. What could these sounds mean? It is midnight; the wind blows gently, and the crew on deck are hardly moving. Yet, I hear a sound, like a human voice, but rougher. It is coming from the cabin where Frankenstein's remains lie. I must get up and investigate. Good night, my sister.

Dear God! The scene that just unfolded is still spinning in my head. I'm not sure if I will be able to explain it, but it is necessary to complete the tale I have written. This final and incredible catastrophe must be shared.

350 I approached the cabin where my unfortunate and admirable friend's remains lay. A figure loomed over him that I struggle to put into words; it was enormous in size, yet strange and distorted in its proportions. As this figure leaned over the coffin, its face was hidden by long, unkempt hair. However, one massive hand reached out, resembling the color and texture of a mummy. When the figure heard me approaching, it stopped expressing grief and horror and abruptly moved towards the window. I have never seen such a horrifying sight as its face, so repulsive yet disturbingly terrifying. I involuntarily closed my eyes and tried to remember how I should handle this destroyer. I called out to it, urging it to stay.

It paused, looking at me with astonishment. Then, it turned back towards the lifeless body of its creator, seeming to forget my presence. Every feature and movement appeared driven by an uncontrolled fury.

"He is also my victim!" it exclaimed. "In his murder, my crimes reach their conclusion. The miserable sequence of my existence is nearing its end! Oh, Frankenstein! You selfless and devoted being! What does it matter now if I plead for your forgiveness? I, who ultimately destroyed you by destroying everything you cherished. Alas! He is cold, unable to respond to me."

351 His voice sounded choked, and I hesitated in carrying out my initial instinct to fulfill my friend's dying wish and destroy his enemy. Instead, a mix of curiosity and pity held me back. I cautiously approached the enormous creature, unable to bring myself to meet his eyes due to the repulsive and otherworldly sight of his ugliness. I tried to speak, but the words died on my lips. The monster continued to babble incoherently, overwhelmed with self-blame. Finally, in a momentary lull in the storm of his emotions, I found the courage to address him: "Your remorse," I said, "is now unnecessary. If you had

listened to your conscience and felt remorse earlier, before resorting to this diabolical revenge, Frankenstein would still be alive."

"You think I was without agony and remorse?" the monster replied, his voice filled with disbelief. "He," he said, pointing to the corpse, "he did not suffer even a fraction of the anguish that tore at me during the long process of carrying out the deed. A terrible self-ishness drove me forward, while my heart was poisoned with remorse. Do you believe that Clerval's groans brought me pleasure? My heart was made to feel love and compassion, and when forced into misery, hatred took over, inflicting a torment unimaginable to you."

"After I murdered Clerval, I returned to Switzerland, completely devastated and overwhelmed with sadness. I felt sorry for Franken-stein, but that pity turned into horror as I despised myself. However, when I discovered that he, the one responsible for my existence and the unimaginable torment it brought, dared to seek happiness for himself, I felt an overwhelming mix of envy and anger. While he accumulated misery and despair upon me, he selfishly pursued his own enjoyment of emotions and experiences that I could never have. This filled me with an unstoppable yearning for revenge. I remem-bered the threat I made and decided that I would carry it out. I knew that I was subjecting myself to a deadly agony, but I had no control over the impulse that I despised, yet could not resist. And yet, when she died!—no, at that moment I was not unhappy. I had discarded all emotions and suppressed all anguish to fully indulge in my boundless despair. Evil became my only solace. Pushed to this point, I had no choice but to adapt my nature to the darkness I willingly chose. Fulfilling my demonic plan became an insatiable obsession. And now, it is finished; there lies my final victim!"

At first, I felt sorry for him and his sadness. But then I remem-bered what Frankenstein had said about his persuasive skills, and when I looked at my friend's lifeless body again, I became angry. "You monster!" I exclaimed. "It's convenient for you to come here and cry over the destruction that you caused. You started the fire, watched everything burn down, and now you sit among the ruins, pretending to be remorseful. You hypocrite! If the person you mourned was still alive, they would still be your target, and you would seek revenge on them again. You're not feeling pity, you're only lamenting because the victim of your wickedness is no longer within your reach."

354   "Oh, it's not like that at all," interrupted the creature. "But I understand how you could think that based on what I've done. However, I am not seeking sympathy for my misery. I don't expect to find any understanding or compassion. When I first looked for sympathy, it was because I wanted to share the love of virtuous feelings, happiness, and affection that filled my entire being. But now, virtue has become a mere illusion to me, and happiness and affection have turned into bitter despair and disgust. So where should I look for sympathy now? I am willing to suffer alone for as long as my suffering lasts. When I die, I am okay with being remembered with abhorrence and contempt. I used to have dreams of virtue, fame, and joy. I used to hope to find beings who would overlook my outward appearance and love me for the good qualities I possessed. I was filled with noble thoughts of honor and devotion. But now, I have been degraded by my crimes to a level lower than even the smallest animal. No guilt, harm, malice, or misery can compare to mine. When I reflect on the terrible list of my sins, I cannot believe that I am the same creature who once had thoughts of grand visions of goodness and its beauty and greatness. But it is true; the fallen angel has become a wicked devil. Even that enemy of God and man had friends and companions in his despair; I am completely alone."

355   You, who consider Frankenstein your friend, seem to know about my wrongdoings and his misfortunes. However, in the account he provided you, he could not fully convey the long periods of suffering I endured, consumed by helpless emotions. While I shattered his dreams, I did not fulfill my own desires. They were always intense and yearning; I still longed for love and companionship, and I was still rejected. Is there no unfairness in this? Am I to be seen as the

only one at fault, when all of humanity acted against me? Why do you not despise Felix, who cast out his friend with disdain at his doorstep? Why do you not condemn the common man who attempted to destroy the rescuer of his child? No, these individuals are considered virtuous and flawless beings! I, the woeful and forsaken one, am an unwanted creation, to be rejected, scorned, and trampled upon. Even now, my anger simmers at the memory of this injustice.

But it is true that I am a terrible person. I have killed innocent and defenseless people. I have taken the lives of those who never harmed me or anyone else. I have made my creator, who is supposed to represent all that is good and worthy of love and admiration, suffer greatly. I have relentlessly pursued them until they met a tragic end. They now lie, lifeless and pale. You may despise me, but your hatred cannot match the self-loathing that consumes me. I look at my own hands, the ones that committed these horrible acts. I think about the twisted thoughts that led me to do such things, and I yearn for the day when I no longer have to face this guilt.

"Do not fear that I will continue to cause harm. I am close to finishing my work. I do not need your death or anyone else's to complete my purpose; only my own is necessary. Rest assured, I will not hesitate to make this sacrifice. I will leave your vessel on the ice-raft that brought me here and venture to the farthest reaches of the North. There, I will gather the materials for my funeral pyre and reduce this wretched body to ashes. I do not want even a trace of me to remain for any curious and unholy person to use as a blueprint. I will die. I will no longer feel the torment that currently engulfs me or be driven by unfulfilled, yet unquenchable, emotions. The one who brought me into existence is already dead, and once I am gone, the memory of both of us will fade quickly. I will no longer see the sun or stars, or feel the wind against my face. Light, sensation, and aware-ness will fade away, and that will be my only source of happiness. Some years ago, when I first experienced the wonders of this world, when I felt the comforting warmth of summer and heard the sounds of rustling leaves and singing birds, those things meant everything to me. I would have mourned my own death. Now, it is my only solace. Stained by my crimes and tormented by the greatest remorse, death is the only place I can find peace."

Goodbye! I'm leaving you, and you are the last human I will ever see with my own eyes. Goodbye, Frankenstein! If you were still alive and still sought revenge against me, it would be better satisfied while I'm alive rather than in my destruction. But that's not the case. You wanted me gone so I wouldn't cause more suffering. And if, by some unknown means, you still think and feel, you wouldn't desire a vengeance greater than what I feel. Though you were devastated, my agony was even worse, because the sharp pain of remorse will continue to hurt me until death closes my wounds forever.

"But soon," he said with sadness and conviction, "I will die, and what I feel now won't be felt anymore. These unbearable sufferings will be gone. I will proudly ascend my funeral pyre and rejoice in the tormenting flames. The light of that fire will fade, and my ashes will be carried away by the wind into the sea. My spirit will rest peacefully, or if it continues to think, it certainly won't think like this. Goodbye."

As he said these words, he jumped out of the cabin window onto the nearby ice raft. The waves quickly carried him away, and he disappeared into the darkness and distance.

THE END.